EYE

OF THE

STORM

A Hart & Drake Thriller

CJ LYONS

ALSO BY CJ LYONS:

Lucy Guardino FBI Thrillers:
SNAKE SKIN
BLOOD STAINED
KILL ZONE
AFTER SHOCK
HARD FALL
BAD BREAK

Hart and Drake Medical Suspense:
NERVES OF STEEL
SLEIGHT OF HAND
FACE TO FACE
EYE OF THE STORM

Shadow Ops Covert Thrillers:
CHASING SHADOWS
LOST IN SHADOWS
EDGE OF SHADOWS

Fatal Insomnia Medical Thrillers:
FAREWELL TO DREAMS
A RAGING DAWN

BORROWED TIME
LUCIDITY: A GHOST OF A LOVE STORY
BROKEN
WATCHED
FIGHT DIRTY

Angels of Mercy Medical Suspense:
LIFELINES
WARNING SIGNS
URGENT CARE
CRITICAL CONDITION

Caitlyn Tierney FBI Thrillers:
BLIND FAITH
BLACK SHEEP
HOLLOW BONES

PRAISE FOR NEW YORK TIMES AND USA TODAY BESTSELLER CJ LYONS:

"Everything a great thriller should be—action packed, authentic, and intense."
~#1 *New York Times* bestselling author Lee Child

"A compelling new voice in thriller writing...I love how the characters come alive on every page." ~*New York Times* bestselling author Jeffery Deaver

"Top Pick! A fascinating and intense thriller." ~ 4 1/2 stars, *RT Book Reviews*

"An intense, emotional thriller...(that) climbs to the edge of intensity." ~*National Examiner*

"A perfect blend of romance and suspense. My kind of read." ~#1 *New York Times* Bestselling author Sandra Brown

"Highly engaging characters, heart-stopping scenes...one great rollercoaster ride that will not be stopping anytime soon." ~Bookreporter.com

"Adrenalin pumping." ~*The Mystery Gazette*

"Riveting." ~*Publishers Weekly Beyond Her Book*

Lyons "is a master within the genre." ~*Pittsburgh Magazine*

"Will leave you breathless and begging for more." ~Romance Novel TV

"A great fast-paced read....Not to be missed." ~4 ƛ Stars, Book Addict

"Breathtakingly fast-paced." ~*Publishers Weekly*

"Simply superb...riveting drama...a perfect ten." ~Romance Reviews Today

"Characters with beating hearts and three dimensions." ~*Newsday*

"A pulse-pounding adrenalin rush!" ~Lisa Gardner

"Packed with adrenalin." ~David Morrell

"...Harrowing, emotional, action-packed and brilliantly realized." ~Susan Wiggs

EYE

OF THE

STORM

A Hart & Drake Thriller

CJ LYONS

Chapter 1

The Security Guard was surprised to see her there. All alone.

He remembered checking her into the Fairstone Museum. She had arrived early, before the rush of limos and Town Cars, accompanied by the tall guy in the off-white dinner jacket and black tie—he remembered because this crowd was strictly into monkey suits. The Artist, the guard thought. They were the only ones who ever arrived early.

At least Mr. Dinner Jacket seemed to have some class. At the last opening, the Artist had arrived in surfer shorts, sporting roach clips and a heroin spoon as jewelry. The crowd loved that, talked all night about his "free spirit" and unwillingness to be "caged by conformity." The guard rolled his eyes at the memory. What a crock. The guy was merely stoned out of his gourd. From the looks of his so-called art, piles of sand with twigs and dog crap stuck in them, drugs were his main source of inspiration as well.

The guard fidgeted, one hand smoothing his hair over the bald spot on top of his head. He looked out into the glass-walled atrium—itself a piece of art with its never-ending springtime of colorful blooms, songbirds, and butterflies that even now, three days before Christmas, kept the Pittsburgh winter at bay. Why was she out there alone? Did she and Mr. Dinner Jacket have a fight? Maybe he should see if she needed anything.

She sat, knees hugged to her chest, the long, purple dress flowing away from her body in streams of color, and curled her bare feet into the luscious carpet of grass. Eggplant, the guard thought, that's what his wife would call the color of her dress. It didn't look like the color of a vegetable, not to him. It reminded him of those ancient sailors, the Phoenicians; the Discovery Channel had just done a special on them; he'd liked the way their ships seemed to fly over the water. They had a special purple dye reserved for royalty—that's what color her dress was.

He glanced at his watch. It was getting late, everyone was here already. Should he tell her? Maybe she didn't want to go inside and face the guy? He could call her a cab, help her get back home.

The guard sighed and stopped his futile fantasies. Seven years of watching couples drift in and out of the gallery, seeing the effect beautiful and powerful art had on them, he recognized true emotion when he saw it.

There was no fight, no reason for him to rescue her. He'd seen the look she'd given her escort, the way the man's hand never strayed far from her body—not out of possessiveness, but compelled by tender regard.

She watched the antics of a hummingbird attracted to the day lilies. Then she smiled. His breath caught. This was no damsel in distress, but if she had been, he would have gladly slain a dragon or two for a chance to see that smile. It wasn't that she was beautiful; her skin was too pale, hair unruly like a child's, eyes a touch too wide and deeply set to be comforting. And her smile was a little cock-eyed, lopsided even.

But there was just something about her. The same something that most of these society women paid their surgeons and cosmetologists dearly for but never achieved. He watched her rise and walk barefoot across the grass toward him. Her dress was sleeveless, falling in drapes down her chest and much lower in the back. He slid off his stool and moved to open the heavy glass door for her as she crossed back into the lobby.

"Thank you."

She wasn't going to tip him for holding the door for her. But he didn't mind. She strode past, her deep purple dress swishing against bare skin. No, he didn't mind at all. He knew instinctively she wasn't like the other women who attended these galas, women who brushed their bodies and hands against him as they waited for husbands to return with the car. Women who acted as if their five-dollar tips had bought and paid for him, who didn't recognize that not everyone had a price.

He watched her bend forward, set black leather heels into place on the gold marble floor, and he sucked in his breath as the folds of her dress shifted over her back, tantalizing him with possibilities.

She rose in one fluid motion and curled her toes before stepping into the shoes. His sigh resonated with hers, echoing against the glass walls of the lobby. He admired the view as she continued down the hall, heels clicking against the marble floor.

She was graceful, but not rigid like a dancer, he thought, hypnotized by the fabric swinging back and forth at her lower back. When he was young, he'd seen a group of Chinese acrobats. One of the set pieces had been two men dueling with sharp swords, one in each hand. The four blades moved faster and faster until they became a blur dancing around the stage. The only thing that prevented bloodshed had been the acrobats' grace, balance, and supreme confidence.

She disappeared into the main gallery and the guard sighed once more, longing for something he'd never possessed in the first place. He gave thanks to God for the mysteries that were women.

His finger tapped the guest list; it was easy to find her name, she and her escort had been the first to arrive. Hart,

Cassandra Hart.

The guard moved back to his desk. He had the sudden urge to talk to his wife, to hear the voice that had kept him company for the past eleven years.

CHAPTER 2

·—₊╫══◄●▶◘◄●▶══╫₊—·

"So, how does it feel to finally come out of the closet?" Jimmy Dolan handed Drake a flute of champagne and grinned at the blush that colored the younger man's cheeks. Always one to push a joke as far as it would go, Jimmy caught the eye of a busty matron swathed in black velvet and diamonds. He leaned over, smacked his lips against Drake's cheek.

"It's all right," he told the woman, wrapping his arm around Drake's shoulder, "we're partners."

"You two make a lovely couple." She gave them an indulgent smile and continued past.

Indeed they did. Drake at six feet was a few inches shorter than Jimmy. His dark hair hung over the collar of his dinner jacket, but Jimmy saw that even though Drake hadn't made it to the barber, he had managed a real bow tie.

Despite his own clip-on tie and military buzz cut, Jimmy thought he still looked pretty damn sophisticated in his black tuxedo. He figured it had something to do with the way his broad shoulders strained against the fabric, making the rental appear custom-fit. The guy at the shop said he was lucky to find one his size.

Drake shrugged his partner's arm away and elbowed Jimmy in the gut. "Would you shut up?"

"What? She loved it, probably thinks she's just so broad-minded now."

Drake rolled his eyes as Jimmy's wife, Denise, approached. "Are you still torturing him?" she chided her husband. "You know, this is why I never take you anywhere."

"Just trying to keep the kid's cover from getting blown. You know everyone thinks these arteests," Jimmy drawled the word, "are all gay. Especially with a name like Remy Michel."

"What did you expect me to use? Pittsburgh Police Detective Rembrandt Michael Drake—specializing in pastels, oils, murder and mayhem?" Drake kept his voice low as they eased into the reception hall.

"You keep pulling in 1.2 million with every sale and you won't need us peons in the Major Case Squad anymore," Jimmy told his partner.

Drake shook his head. 1.2 million. Hearing it aloud

made his ears ring. Last week when he'd gotten the check and held it, he'd actually felt his knees sag. Not because of how much money it was—but because someone would pay that kind of money for something he'd painted, for an original Drake—or Remy Michel to use his *nom de l'art*. It was exhilarating.

And it scared the crap out of him. What if he never created anything that good again? What if *Steadfast* was a fluke—a one-hit wonder? He'd been painting for years; sales of his work in galleries on the East Coast had been modest but steady. Encouraging was the adjective his manager used.

But 1.2 million? Only a family like the Fairstones would have that kind of money to blow on three canvases. Although, Drake thought with a smile, it wasn't as if they weren't getting their money's worth. The model for the triptych was exceptionally inspiring.

He just wished Alicia Fairstone hadn't been from Pittsburgh. She'd insisted on learning the true name of the artist she'd selected to grace the new headquarters of her charitable foundation. He'd always kept his art separate and anonymous from his life as a detective on the Pittsburgh Police Bureau's Major Case Squad. Never even told Jimmy, his partner of five years, until a few weeks ago when the Fairstones announced they were going to display *Steadfast* as part of their annual holiday fundraising gala. Even now, Jimmy was the only cop who knew about Drake's second career.

"Where's Hart?" he asked Denise. He had thought the two women had gone to the ladies' room together, to do whatever it was that took women so long in bathrooms.

"Cassie's a little nervous. She's afraid everyone will recognize her as the model."

"With a body like hers, she's got nothing to be ashamed about," Jimmy said, earning simultaneous elbows to the gut from both of his partners.

"You better not talk like that around her," Denise told him.

"How would you know anyway?" Drake asked.

Jimmy gave a heaving sigh. "A man can dream, can't he?"

Denise merely arched an eyebrow at him. It was the same look she gave their kids when they were pushing her limits. Jimmy straightened up with alacrity. The mother of twin six-year-olds, Denise stayed trim in the natural course of days spent chasing them both. Not to mention the effort it took to keep her husband in line and run a business as a financial consultant.

"How're we doing on money?" Drake asked her. 1.2 million sounded like a lot, but after the government and his manager took their share, there wasn't much left. Not to mention the final payment on renovations to convert the part of his building into a community clinic, the Liberty Center.

Denise frowned. "It's a good thing the check cleared," she told him. "That money's already spent."

Easy come, easy go. Creating a nonprofit and getting it up and running was taking more time, money, and effort than he ever imagined. But it was a helluva lot of fun—almost as good as painting or nailing a criminal. Plus, it gave him a chance to work side by side with Hart.

A black woman with voluptuous curves accentuated by her gold, form-fitting dress approached.

"Where's Cassie?" Adeena Coleman was Hart's best friend and a social worker helping out at the Liberty Center. "Let me guess. She's hiding." She shook her head, her intricate arrangement of beaded braids swinging with the movement.

"I was just going to look for her." Drake left them mingling with Pittsburgh's rich and famous. He worked his way through the crowd, searching each of the museum's smaller galleries until he came to one that was dimly lit and quiet. The walls were draped in indigo velvet while flood lights illuminated sculptures of ivory and bronze.

His breath caught when he spotted the alabaster figure of a woman standing beside one of Degas' dancers, her back to him. Her shoulders were draped in a low cascade of fabric that revealed the sinuous curves of her back as well as the well-defined muscles of her shoulders. She balanced with her weight on one bare foot, the arch of her other foot curving up her calf as if she were a ballet dancer preparing for an arabesque.

The foot moved up and down, winking in and out of folds of aubergine velvet, offering Drake enticing views of skin. Then she shifted her weight and stepped back into her heels.

Dr. Cassandra Hart made the sound of a woman whose feet were suffering dearly in the cause of fashion and love. She turned to look over her shoulder.

Her dark, almond-shaped eyes met Drake's and her mouth rounded in the O of a child caught shaking Christmas presents. The unruly curls she'd tried to restrain in a French braid had escaped, twisting in tendrils around her face.

She wore no stockings, no makeup, and no jewelry other than a small sapphire ring on the third finger of her left hand. To Drake, she was the most beautiful thing in this gallery filled with masterpieces. He moved forward, handed her his champagne to sip, and wrapped one arm around her waist.

"They'll be starting soon," he told her. She leaned back into him, and he could feel the tension knotting her muscles. Unless it was in the midst of managing a multiple trauma, Hart hated crowds.

Yet still she came tonight, to be with Drake in his hour of triumph. Hart believed actions spoke louder than words and this one spoke volumes to Drake.

She said nothing, taking a quick gulp of champagne to steel her nerves.

"Have I told you how beautiful you look tonight?" He turned her in his arms so she faced him.

Steadfast was the first major piece he'd finished since

he met her ten months ago, the first since he'd been shot and almost died before she saved him, the first inspired by Hart.

He leaned forward to kiss her deeply. If he never raised a brush again, it was enough, *this* was enough. He wouldn't trade this simple woman or her quiet beauty for all the diamonds in the building.

"It'll be all right." He took her by the hand and led her back to the reception hall.

"Detective Drake!" A woman in her early forties, her blond hair pulled back into a tight bun, the better to display the diamond and ruby earrings that matched the heavy necklace draped over her ample bust, waved a hand.

Drake cringed at the use of his real name, but knew he couldn't avoid her. Alicia Fairstone was the hostess of tonight's festivities and thus, considered herself Drake's patroness. He had asked her not to announce his presence at the opening. In the program he was listed as Remy Michel, a local artist, with no biographic information.

Before he could beat a retreat, Alicia was in front of them, extending her slender, manicured hand to Drake.

He hid his sigh in a gracious smile and lifted the hand to brush his lips.

"Isn't it marvelous, Detective?" Alicia gushed, snaking her arm around his even as she raked Hart with an appraising look. The Fairstone heiress had already disposed of husbands one and two and was rumored to be on the prowl for number three.

"Please, Ms. Fairstone," Drake said.

"I'm so sorry. I forgot that you were undercover, so to speak. Then I shall call you Remy and you may call me Alicia. That way your secret will be safe." She turned to Hart. "And you brought your model with you—how thoughtful of you, Remy."

Alicia unleashed him long enough to take both of Hart's hands into hers. "My dear, you're much too thin," she said. "I hope these scars aren't marks of that 'cutting' thing that I've heard some models do. You aren't anorexic, are you? Because we've laid out a sumptuous buffet."

The socialite steered Hart away from Drake and toward the food. Drake felt compelled to intervene. Not for Hart's sake, but Alicia's. Hart wore her "wither and die" look and Alicia had no idea who she was dealing with. Just as the heiress didn't realize that Hart had earned the ragged scar on her left arm, along with several others, while struggling with a serial killer. Alicia was also oblivious to the fact that, despite Hart's petite frame, she was all compacted muscle—strong enough to spar with men twice her size while earning her Kempo black belt.

He gulped as color suffused Hart's face and she aimed a glare at Alicia's hand on her arm. If he didn't do something soon, he could lose his deep-pocketed patroness. Which was something they couldn't afford.

"May I present Dr. Cassandra Hart?" Drake said, inserting himself between the two women. "This is Alicia Fairstone, who purchased *Steadfast.* She's arranged for the

Liberty Center to receive the proceeds from the silent auction later tonight."

Hart darted a look at him; he'd be paying later for her self-control. She disengaged her hands from Alicia's. "That's very kind of you," she said through gritted teeth.

"I'm always looking for worthy causes to invest in." Alicia linked her arm through Drake's once more. "If an artist of Remy's caliber supports the Liberty Center, then it must be a good cause." She brushed her free hand over Drake's arm possessively. "I feel quite proud to have discovered him. After tonight, Remy, you can quit your day job and concentrate on your art full time."

Like hell, Drake thought. Alicia obviously hadn't gotten a recent look at his checkbook. Besides, he loved being a cop—who would want to give that up?

Chapter 3

"Certainly Remy should be able to pay you more for your time," Alicia continued, her gaze moving over Cassie's dress. "What's your doctorate in? Art History? It's so difficult to get a job in academics these days."

Cassie blushed with embarrassment as she realized Alicia must know exactly how much her dress cost: $229.98 on Macy's clearance rack of prom and wedding rejects. A significant investment since she was no longer employed other than her full-time volunteer work with the Liberty Center.

"You will excuse us, won't you?" Alicia went on, already pulling Drake away. "I've some people for you to meet, Remy. Important people who will be invaluable to advancing your career."

Cassie watched them move away and finished Drake's champagne in a single gulp. She knew it was all playacting on behalf of a good cause, but, dammit, Drake didn't have to be enjoying it so much. She bit her lip as he laughed at one of Alicia's jokes—probably something terribly witty and urbane—and then tensed as his hand reached up to stroke the other woman's shoulder.

She hadn't realized she'd taken a step forward until a meaty hand clamped onto her arm.

"Not so fast," Jimmy Dolan told her. He nodded toward his partner and the small but growing crowd of society women, all fawning over Drake, their poses designed to be enticing, hands on hips, busts thrust out to reveal the best cosmetic surgery money could buy.

Drake laughed again, and Cassie almost snapped the stem of her glass in two. Jimmy pried the crystal from her and handed it to a passing waiter. "They're auditioning to be his next model."

"They can have the job," she muttered.

"Just watch," he ordered in his best ex-marine drill sergeant tone.

Drake continued to entertain, a peacock surrounded by a bevel of well-heeled peahen. He flicked a smile in Cassie's direction and winked. She held her impulse to stick her tongue out at him, then covered her mouth with her hand to hide her grin as Drake's hand sidled down Alicia's back. His fingers deftly twisted the label of her designer gown so it hung garishly above the black velvet.

"You should know better," Jimmy reproved her, but he was smiling as well. He saluted his fellow officer's sleight of hand. "C'mon, let's get some free food before all the rich people gobble it up."

They left Drake to hold his own with the female barracudas and tackled the buffet. Jimmy guided her to a table in the rear where they joined Denise and Adeena.

"Thanks for the rescue," Cassie told him before she settled into her dinner.

"No problem, I was ready for seconds anyway."

Denise reached over to pat the expanse of stomach above his cummerbund. "You may want to rethink that. More calories to work off later."

Jimmy lifted her hand and nibbled his way down her arm. Denise giggled. "I know the best fat-burning calisthenics around," he said with a leer and then whispered in her ear.

"Stop." She swatted him away. "I'm trying to eat here."

Cassie watched the couple resume eating, their free hands intertwined. Jimmy and Denise were high school sweethearts, married before he joined the Marines, happy now for over twenty years. She glanced up as Drake entered the dining area, Alicia Fairstone draped over him like a mink stole. As he walked, he scanned the room, the candlelight transforming his blue eyes into twinkling sapphires. Then those eyes locked onto hers and it was as if they were standing together, face-to-face, instead of separated by thirty feet and a hundred strangers.

He smiled at her. She had to remind herself to breathe. They'd known each other for not quite a year and had been through a lot. Yet, she still got the same nervous flip-flop in her stomach she'd gotten the first time he'd looked at her that way. Her toes curled out of her pumps, too excited to remain confined by the tight leather.

She felt the color rise to her face and forgot her fork in midair, overwhelmed with the knowledge that this was the man she would be marrying in two days. Then Adeena said something to her and she caught herself just before the scallop slid off her fork.

"Sorry, what?" She tore her attention away from Drake with an effort.

DRAKE WATCHED HART from his place at the main table. He would have loved to seat her in the midst of all this store-bought beauty and dazzle these fatuous art lovers with the real thing. It would have been so damned satisfying. But he restrained himself and listened with half an ear as Alicia described her latest cruise to Corfu.

As his hands mechanically forked food and guided it to his mouth, he looked over at the tableau surrounding Hart. Denise sat on one side, her pale features reflecting her Scandinavian and European ancestry. Adeena with her intriguing African regal bearing sat on the other side. With Hart in the middle—a melting pot of many cultures. Her grandmother Rosa had been a gypsy of the Kalderasha clan and had given Hart her almond shaped dark eyes and high cheekbones—a delicious and delightful blend of ancient Persia, Eastern Europe, and the Mediterranean. Hart had a lot of Irish in her as well from her grandfather Padraic Hart, her Hibernian coloring reflecting every change of mood with subtle highlights Drake was learning to read and interpret it like an illuminated manuscript.

He glanced around at the best Pittsburgh society had to offer and felt they, despite their well-documented bloodlines, paled in comparison to the three women across the room.

His fingers twitched and suddenly he knew where his next composition would be drawn from. Hart looked up from something Adeena was saying and smiled, her head thrown back, rambunctious hair threatening revolt from its confines. She didn't laugh; Hart very rarely did, but both Adeena and Denise were, probably at Jimmy's expense, he thought, watching his partner blush and tuck into his food.

Just that—that very moment, the candlelight, the evening clothes, sparkling jewels adorning everyone except Hart, the way her eyes simultaneously conveyed both joy and a serious regard for the moment—that was what he would paint next.

"Is something wrong, Remy?" Alicia interrupted herself to ask.

"No," he assured her. "Everything is fine. I must thank you—you've given me the inspiration for my next painting."

Alicia smiled broadly and preened. "I can't wait to see it."

⁕

THE DINNER WAS interminably long, but finally they were released for the main event. Alicia led the way into the main gallery. Drake rejoined Cassie, his hand searching hers out, asking silently for forgiveness. She relented and gave his fingers a quick squeeze. Alicia made her way up to a small podium. A red velvet curtain shielded the wall behind the podium and the lights were turned up to full.

"Ladies and gentlemen," Alicia started, "I would like to introduce you all to a work of art recently acquired by the Fairstone Foundation. The artist is local, although he regrets that he could not be here with us tonight." She smirked in Drake's direction. "His name is Remy Michel and I'm sure you'll agree he is destined to become a great talent. And now without further ado, I give you *Steadfast.*"

There was a hushed silence. The curtains parted. Cassie tightened her grip on Drake's hand and held her breath, waiting for the audience's reaction. This meant so much to Drake—not just the money but also the approval, the validation that he had true talent. They just had to like it, she prayed, her eyes never leaving Drake's face. His gaze was riveted straight ahead, looking on his work of art as it was unveiled.

Spotlights came up on the three large canvases. They

were hung in a stepwise fashion. The lowest on the left depicted a female figure bowed on one knee, seemingly imprisoned in the earth. Her hair hung over her face, a curtain revealing only the determined set of her jaw. From behind shoulders hunched either by effort or defeat, wings furled tight, almost hidden by her body.

In the middle canvas, the angel began to rise, breaking free from invisible bonds. More of her face could be seen as her wings lifted, began to spread wide. The pigments swirled in a tantalizing mix of the mundane and the glorious, taking on a transparent, gossamer quality. This play of light and color burst forth in the final canvas as the angel stood tall, her face fully revealed in the radiance reflected from her open wings.

Cassie knew the hours Drake had labored on the paintings, the false starts and trials of different pigments and techniques. Through it all she'd begged him to use a better model, a professional, someone who could give him what his work deserved.

Now with his work unveiled, she saw a smile of satisfaction settle onto his face. He squeezed her hand, looked down at her, and she knew it didn't matter what anyone else thought about *Steadfast*. Drake saw in it what he had wanted to convey.

Murmurs of appreciation and admiration began to run through the crowd. "Exquisite." "Marvelous." "Radiant." The same people who'd been filling the air with tales of their latest Wall Street conquests now whispered in the humbled tones of churchgoers.

"Jeezit," came a familiar voice from behind them and the tension was broken as everyone turned to stare at Jimmy Dolan's slack jawed expression of delight.

A round of applause began, led by Alicia Fairstone, who was obviously relieved that her acquisition had been so well received.

The applause was gaining in momentum when the lights suddenly died, throwing the assembly into pitch darkness. The crowd gave a startled gasp. Cassie felt Drake's arm circle around her, snugging her close to him. Before anyone could move, there was a loud pop followed by a whoosh then two more pops in quick succession.

Suddenly, all three canvases were lit by blue-tongued flames that raced across the oils, sending sooty tendrils of smoke over the crowd.

The crowd stood still for one hushed breath, waiting for the punch line to a joke they had missed.

Jimmy, Cassie, and Drake all rushed forward. The rest of the crowd broke and panicked. A shrill scream came from Alicia Fairstone's direction and other women quickly joined in.

Cassie and Drake were separated in the surging crowd. The mob thronged toward the main exit. Cassie pushed past them, heading to the curtains at the side of the stage, intending to pull them down and use them to smother the flames. She'd just reached them when she was knocked to the ground by an elderly man who'd been shoved aside in the mass exodus.

She protected the man with her own body and then helped him to his feet, only to be knocked down once more. As she climbed to her knees, she saw Drake silhouetted by flames, trying to beat them out with his jacket.

"Drake!" She watched in horror as his jacket caught on fire. She reached for the curtains and gave a mighty tug, then one more, popping the drape from its rings.

Cassie bundled the fabric in her arms and rushed toward Drake. He seemed intent on saving his creation, heedless of the fire that now surrounded him. She threw her body at him, tackling him, smothering his arm under the heavy material. He dropped his jacket and tried to push her away.

The whoosh of a fire extinguisher came from beside them. Jimmy aimed the foam over Drake, smothering the remaining flames on his jacket and the curtains. Then he raised the nozzle toward the paintings.

Drake tried to get to his feet, to move forward once more, but Cassie hauled him back, using all her strength. "No," she told him. "They're gone. Give it up. They're gone."

Jimmy emptied the fire extinguisher, coughing in the thick, coiling smoke, and stepped back. Flames still licked the wooden frames, searching for fuel, but the canvases all hung in sickly, swollen, black tatters.

The sounds of a fire alarm shrieked through the air and the emergency lights finally came on. Cassie wished they hadn't when she saw the look of anguish on Drake's face. She'd never seen him in such pain before—not even when he'd been shot.

Jimmy took one arm and Cassie the other. Together, they led Drake in silence from the gallery. Behind them, the last of the flames died, leaving only soot and burnt canvas on the walls.

Steadfast had died a grotesque death, its promise snuffed out just as it was being fulfilled. Drake looked back over his shoulder, still seeing Hart's visage in the three canvases, not wanting to accept the murder of his creation. His eyes absorbed every detail because that was what he did best—better than painting, even.

Drake was a murder cop.

CHAPTER 4

CASSIE HAD DECLINED the offer of a ride from Adeena, who'd left to drive Denise home to relieve their babysitter. They'd all see each other tomorrow at the wedding rehearsal party Adeena was hosting along with her Great Aunt Tessa, who'd been Cassie's grandmother's best friend.

Cassie knew she could be of no help to Drake in sorting out the aftermath of the fire, but if someone had targeted Drake's art, then he was also a target and she didn't intend to stray very far from his side.

Besides, if she left him to his own devices, he'd spend all night here or down at the Zone Seven station house pursuing the case without rest. All without venting any of the anger that had to be building inside of him.

She should know, because although Drake could slam

down his emotions behind an impenetrable vault door, Cassie didn't have that ability. Confusion, fear, resentment, and fury churned through her, building to a crescendo. Why? Why target a piece of art, a thing of beauty? Who would perform such a wanton act of destruction that no one could possibly profit from?

There was no money motive—Drake had been paid, the paintings were insured, only the insurance company lost. Although tonight would undoubtedly propel Drake into the spotlight he detested, his art career would most likely improve. She frowned as she imagined rich benefactors trying to out do themselves as the next one "brave" enough to unveil a Remy Michel work.

Maybe Alicia Fairstone planned it that way? The heiress certainly craved the adoration of the public and her own social group. Would she go so far to stage a publicity coup?

Surely not. But she liked the prospect of seeing Alicia Fairstone jailed for arson and maybe insurance fraud. Cassie stood before a small, delicately brushed Renoir, considering. It was difficult to feel so angry when faced with such beauty.

What had the arsonist felt as he looked upon *Steadfast?* Why hadn't he felt the beauty of Drake's creation? What had fueled the rage that led to his act of destruction?

She gave her statement to one of the police officers ensconced in the gallery's employee lounge. Detectives from

Major Crimes and the Arson squads were using the more lavish executive offices upstairs to interview Pittsburgh's rich and famous.

Drake wouldn't leave the crime scene until he was certain every last detail had been extracted from it—even if officially this wasn't his case. She ducked into the ladies' room, thinking she'd find a little peace and quiet there.

Wrong. Women glittering with jewels thronged the mirrored counters, adjusting their makeup and hair as they recounted the excitement of tonight's events. Cassie listened from the doorway as the tales of heroics and danger grew more and more preposterous. To hear them tell it, they or their brave husbands had each put out the fire with their bare hands.

"That Tony Marinelli from Channel Four is just so cute," one taut-faced brunette crooned as she wiggled her cleavage into a more enticing position. "The police made all the reporters move across the street, but he promised an exclusive interview—said he'd wait for me."

"Honey, that's what he told us all," one of her companions replied as she elbowed for mirror room. "They'll film us then pick and choose the best sound bite."

"Can you believe Alicia's luck?" another voice pitched in. "First, finding those spectacular paintings and then—"

"Hosting an equally spectacular viewing," a world-wise blonde finished for her. She licked her lips and checked her profile. "I heard the artist is the hunky piece of work in the dinner jacket. Talk about spectacular." She slid her hands down, smoothing her dress over her hips.

"I heard he's actually a cop." The first woman giggled. "He can come investigate me anytime."

"Only if he promises a strip search."

Cassie listened to the banter as more women joined them, crowding the lavish facilities. Finally, she jostled to a space in front of a sink and washed her hands and face. The water soon ran black with soot. Silence settled over the room.

A dozen or so eyes stared at her, raking over her dirty appearance and the scorched patches that marred her dress. Abrasions covered her arms and shins from when she tackled Drake. And she'd lost her shoes—at least something good had come from the night.

"And what did you think of tonight's unveiling?" the bitch blonde asked her, hands on her hips. "Don't suppose you and your friend the artist set it up in order to generate commissions, rev up some word of mouth?" The crowd parted as if for a western style gunfight. The blonde stood by the toilet stalls, hands on her hips, ready to draw.

Cassie's lips twisted into a half-smile as she regarded the blonde in the mirror. The towels were all gone, so she shook the water from her face and hands, marring the pristine surface of the mirror and marble topped vanity. And not caring.

Never start a fight, the voice of her grandfather Padraic Hart came to her. But if one comes your way, always, always finish it.

Cassie took a deep breath. It would be too damned easy—almost like picking on a senior citizen, she thought, noticing the wrinkles that even skilled cosmetic application and Botox couldn't hide. And it might cost Drake in the long run.

That reined her in. Used to be she'd let her temper flare, getting the best of her before she'd think twice about it. But that was before she'd met Drake.

Instead, Cassie merely smiled and borrowed a line she'd been dying to use for years. "You talking to me?" she drawled, arching an eyebrow and speaking to the woman's reflection in the mirror.

Before the blonde could answer, Cassie turned and walked away, her bare feet leaving small footprints on the Italian marble.

The door closed behind her and she leaned against the wall, giddy with triumph. She never knew that walking away from a fight could feel almost as good as winning one outright. She'd have to remember that. Hell, maybe she was finally outgrowing her temper. It was about time.

She looked up and was surprised to see she wasn't alone in the corridor. A trim, medium-height, gray-haired man lounged against the opposite wall, regarding her with a knowing gleam in his eyes. He appeared to be in his late-sixties, but his eyes were much, much older. His gaze moved slowly from her head to toes, dark hazel eyes drinking in everything with a voracity that brought a flush to Cassie's face.

She turned to leave, but he moved faster than she guessed he could, reaching a hand to take her left arm. The touch of his skin on hers jolted through the sensitive flesh of her scar and she whirled, yanking her arm from his grasp.

"I'm sorry," he purred in a vaguely European accent. He gestured with his other hand, holding a thick and expensive-looking cigar. "I wondered if smoking was permitted?" His inflection emphasized the question but his gaze held hers with an intensity that made Cassie certain the query wasn't foremost on his mind.

"No, I don't think it is." She took a step away but a shiver on the back of her neck warned her against turning her back on him or running. He grinned like a wolf and pocketed the cigar with regret.

"Ah, dear." He sighed dramatically. She continued to edge away, but he moved toward her with a predator's grace. "You were the angel, no?" he asked, his accent thickening, making Cassie certain he was dramatizing it. "In the beautiful paintings."

She nodded, acknowledging the clench of fear his presence brought to her gut, but refusing to yield to it. Or him.

"And you are?" she asked, trying for the offensive.

He waved off her question as irrelevant. "An admirer. My what a beautiful ring." His fingers lifted her left hand, his thumb stroking her sapphire engagement ring. Cassie felt thick callouses across his palm and noticed he had a strange-shaped scar on the back of his right hand. Smaller, straighter than any of her scars, dagger shaped—too regular for an accidental laceration, she thought as she stared with a clinician's eye. Not surgical either.

A brand? She glanced up and saw he had noted her reaction. She tugged her hand away from his.

"Thank you," she murmured, listening for any other people. All those giddy society matrons in the restroom and not one of them done yet? But the corridor remained stubbornly empty.

Except for Cassie and the wolf-man in front of her. His eyes narrowed and his grin widened as if he read her thoughts. Cassie's weight shifted automatically into a fighting stance and it was all she could do to keep from balling her hands into fists.

"Give Drake my congratulations on your upcoming wedding," the man drawled, his accent mysteriously vanished. He allowed Cassie to back away, remaining in the shadows while she moved toward the lights near the entrance to the restroom. "And my condolences."

With that, he was gone. How did he know Drake? she wondered, but the knot of fear and prickling on the back of her neck convinced her that following him into the shadows would be a mistake.

A big mistake.

She shook her head as the door to the ladies' room opened, disgorging a bevy of jewel-studded women who swarmed around Cassie as she stared at the spot where the man had disappeared.

She allowed the tide of women to carry her to the main entrance. They collected their various spouses and companions and chattered their way through the door and across the street to the restaurant where the TV crews and fifteen minutes of fame awaited.

The coat check staff had already been sent home, leaving all the outerwear on racks, but it was easy to find Cassie's wool coat Drake had bought her after she'd fallen in love with the rich, scarlet color. She grabbed it and rushed out into the night air, hanging the coat over her shoulders like a cape, leaving her arms free. She stopped— where was she going? Nowhere without Drake, but she couldn't stand going back inside, breathing any more of the perfumed air that couldn't mask the stench of ashes.

Other patrons streamed past, a few with sidelong glances in her direction. Ignoring them, she sat down on the steps to the museum, hoping to clear her thoughts.

Should she tell Drake about the man's threat? Except they weren't really threats, were they? Not even insinuations. No. He'd be certain to overreact, want to do something like send her to Antarctica to keep her safe, argue that they were better off separated until any threat was past. Maybe even want to postpone their wedding.

Who was that man? She'd seen that mark on his wrist before—no, no, she'd heard about it. From Gram Rosa. A dagger branded onto the inside of the wrist, the mark of the Lowara. The gypsy clan who had betrayed Rosa and her family to the Nazis back in 1936.

The man wasn't old enough to be a part of that. But on a night like this, artwork targeted, burned for no reason, lives placed at risk, she wondered if somehow the past had pierced the veil of time to target the present.

CHAPTER 5

THE BOY WATCHED the dark-haired woman sitting on the steps without shoes, her coat not even buttoned, yet impervious to the cold. She wasn't like the others, not with the proud carriage to her spine, the way she held her head high. Obviously not a rube. More like a lioness on the prowl. He should ignore her, concentrate on finding another mark before Natasha got angry that he wasn't bringing in his fair share of the night's bounty.

Rich people draped in fur dribbled out the museum doors and down the steps in pairs. They all studiously ignored the woman in the dark, flowing dress, her skin glowing like moonlight. Just as Vincent should have.

Natasha would have his hide for allowing so many potential targets pass by. But he couldn't take his eyes off her. The woman was just another *gaje*; what made her so special anyway? She didn't have any of the sparkling jewelry or soft furs of the other women who exited the gala. Plus, she was alone, which should have made her especially vulnerable.

Instead, her aloneness seemed to empower her, as if she possessed the strength to create her own reality and carry it with her, surround herself with herself, shutting out the ugly reality of the world beyond.

Vincent was irresistibly drawn to that power, wanted to learn it for himself. He took a step toward the woman, was halfway to her before he realized his mistake. His attraction had alerted the others. Suddenly, Natasha appeared before the woman as if conjured from the dark night.

Conjured forth from hell was more like it, the boy thought, trying to hurry without appearing concerned as the old woman took his lady's hands into hers.

Natasha pulled his lady to her feet. His lady was short enough that even though she stood on a step higher than Natasha's, they stood eye to eye.

Vincent arrived at her side, breathless with anticipation and fear as Natasha brought one of his lady's hands to her heart, pulling his lady close as the others gathered silently behind her.

"Let me offer my services. I can glimpse into the shadows of your future," Natasha crooned, swaying hypnotically, pulling his lady with her.

This was their cue and the others to begin to lightly race their fingers over the woman's body, searching every nook and crevice of her clothing for valuables. Usually the mark had his eyes closed by now and felt the children's light touch as palpable manifestations of Natasha's psychic powers. Natasha's banter was designed to encourage this as well.

"The spirits hover all around you," she intoned, pulling the woman back and forth, the better to access inner pockets and purses.

To Vincent's astonishment his lady—he knew she was no mark—merely laughed, shrugging off the searching hands.

"I don't have anything," she said, her voice clear and without anger. He'd never heard a *gaje* speak like that, especially not one who caught them in their act of larceny.

Natasha started, her face filling with anger, eyes blazing into his lady's. His lady merely smiled, cementing forever her place in Vincent's heart. No one could stand up to Natasha, at least no one that he knew. Not even Nickolai, the Royal, the leader of their little family.

The others stepped back into the shadows, the better to retreat and flee. But Vincent continued forward, circling to stand close by his lady, as if a twelve-year-old boy could offer her any protection from Natasha's wrath.

His lady's eyes gave her away—wide, dark eyes that looked into Natasha's without flinching. The eyes of a Rom, deep, challenging, refusing to yield.

She shifted her weight slightly and he saw with amazement that it was she who now held Natasha's hands. She lifted the witch's left palm to her breast, resting it over her heart, pinning it there despite the older woman's desperate squirming. Then she rotated Natasha's right hand palm up.

"Perhaps I should read your future," she suggested.

Natasha tried and failed to pull away. "*Marhime gaje!*" the curse emerged in a shrill, choked voice that was very much unlike Natasha's usual barks of commands. "Who are you?" the witch snarled.

"My name isn't important. My grandmother was Rosa Costello of the Kalderasha."

Natasha froze. "That's impossible."

Vincent stared up at the two, mesmerized by the contest of wills. Sparks of power seemed to fill the night around them and he felt a chill settle over his body.

They're just fireflies, he told himself. But fireflies had never scared him so much that his entire body trembled. And how to explain fireflies appearing in the midst of a Pittsburgh December?

Vincent wasn't afraid of anything, he told himself, forcing his body to stand straight and tall. None of the family were.

Finally Natasha found her voice. "Rosa was killed. During the War. All of her *kumpania* as well."

"Rosa's family was betrayed. A Lowara told the Nazis about their campsite location in exchange for all their wagons and horses. Everyone knows the Lowara are thieves, only one step up from *gaje*."

"I'm Lowara," Natasha declared, her courage returning as she finally broke free of his lady's grip. Or did Rosa's granddaughter let her go? Vincent rather thought so, watching Natasha massage her sore wrists.

"I know."

"Then you also know that Lowara are the best knife wielders alive. And we don't take kindly to accusations from *marhime*!" Natasha spat at his lady.

Instead of distracting his lady and allowing Natasha to draw her knife, his lady ignored the spittle sliding down her cheek, and in a lightning move, twisted the knife free of Natasha's hand as soon as it cleared her skirt pocket.

"The Rom turned their backs on my grandmother after she saved many of them from the Nazis. She was declared unclean, *marhime*. Many of the Lowara alive today owe their lives to my grandmother. Perhaps I will collect on the debt someday."

"If you try, you'll die," Natasha hissed.

Vincent swelled with pride as his lady merely laughed and thrust her upturned palm into Natasha's face. "Look again, old woman. Better than you have tried and failed."

The lights from the museum glistened as they danced across a heaped-up scar shaped like a crescent moon that swirled around the base of her thumb. Her left arm, which held the knife in a deceptively casual fashion, also carried a scar, this one jagged like the tail of a serpent—or a dragon.

A sudden gust of wind shivered through him.

Natasha looked down, drawn against her will, and Vincent heard her sharp intake of breath. Then she looked up into his lady's eyes. Natasha dropped his lady's hand as if it burnt her and clattered down the steps, running into the night.

His lady watched her go, idly twirling the knife in her hand. Then she turned her dark gaze on Vincent.

"Something I can do for you?" she asked. Her voice radiated through him like light spiraling through a crystal.

Vincent only nodded, taking her right hand and looking down into its depths himself. He saw nothing there but furrowed lines and the heaped skin of the scar. He knew he did not have the gift to read others like Natasha, but still, he was disappointed. He looked into his lady's eyes and lifted her palm, caressing her scar with his lips.

She surprised him with a quick smile that lit the darkness around him, banishing all fear. He bowed over her hand. "I am Vincent," he said, feeling much older than he was. "Please call upon me in your need, my lady."

She nodded gravely, accepting his offer. "I'm Cassandra Hart. Do you know anything about what happened here tonight, Vincent? About the fire?"

He did. Just as he knew Natasha's surprise at meeting Rosa Costello's granddaughter had been an act. But he couldn't betray his family—Nickolai would kill him if he said anything. Vincent bowed once more and then turned and ran, his legs pumping with nervous energy, skipping him down the steps two at a time. Cassandra Hart lifted her left hand in a small wave before turning and climbing the steps back to the marble halls of the *gaje* world.

That's when Vincent realized her left hand was empty, but where was the knife? It wasn't on the steps, he saw. He put his hands on his hips and felt the bone hilt. She'd slid it into his belt. Vincent drew it slowly, carefully. Natasha's blade—now his. All that wonder, power—his.

His fingers closed over the hilt and he vowed to use the knife only to protect his lady from evil—like the revenge he was certain Natasha was already plotting.

CHAPTER 6

When Cassie returned inside, she found Drake standing with Jimmy and a man dressed in a navy polo shirt, tan sports jacket, and khaki pants, his posture proclaiming his membership in the law enforcement fraternity. Drake had rolled up his shirtsleeves and his black tie dangled from his unbuttoned shirt collar. Jimmy still wore his tuxedo jacket but his hand kept going to tug at his collar and tie and Cassie knew he was searching for any excuse to pull it free. He caught her gaze and lowered his hand with a guilty smile. Denise must have given him strict instructions about tending to expensive rental suits.

Cassie moved to join the group, both Jimmy and Drake automatically making room for her in their circle as if she were an equal. The third man looked up at her with annoyance, stopping his speech at her arrival.

"One of the uniformed officers can take your statement, ma'am," he told her in a frosty tone, his gaze following the arc of the black leather pumps that Drake dangled on the tips of two fingers and passed to her. "This room is off limits."

Cassie reluctantly accepted the shoes. She ignored the detective to peer at a diagram Drake was holding. It appeared to be a device consisting of a small electronic apparatus connected to an elongated vial shaped like a large light bulb.

"Cassie, this is Detective Romero, arson squad," Jimmy made introductions, suppressing his grin at Romero's discomfort over the presence of a civilian.

"Remote control?" Cassie asked. She looked up at Romero. "Something that produced a spark or electrical current?"

The arson detective nodded grudgingly. "Remote car starter. The trigger would look like a car alarm key fob."

"What kind of flammable liquid was it? I couldn't smell anything but it burned fast."

Romero pursed his lips, obviously determined not to allow a civilian further into his confidence. Drake answered for her.

"Lamp oil mixed with paraffin. The heat of the current burst the light bulbs and simultaneously ignited it as it poured down over the canvas."

"The pops we heard." He nodded. "Who knew far

enough ahead of time to set them up? It had to be someone who knew you were the artist."

Romero shoved his hands into his pants pockets, his jacket opening to display his gun and badge—reminders of who was in charge here. "What makes you think Ms. Fairstone wasn't the intended victim? She's the one out a million dollars worth of art."

"Not after the insurance pays. And while this might not be the most successful fund raiser of the season, it will certainly by the most memorable and talked about." Cassie shook her head. "The only losers here were Drake and the clinic. The bastard could have at least waited until after the auction."

❦

DRAKE CUT HER a look accompanied by a half smile. Leave it to Hart to get her priorities straight, he thought. He could always depend on her to slice through the bullshit.

Romero made a small noise and Drake realized the detective had just put two and two together and figured out who Hart was.

"How can you be so certain you weren't the target, Dr. Hart?" Romero asked, his tone indicating he was tired of playing games. "I understand your ex-husband's brother was here tonight?"

Drake glanced up at that. Alan King would definitely top his list of anyone with a grudge against Hart—and

Drake. "King was here?"

"I didn't see him," Hart said. "If Alan King wanted revenge over his brother's death, he'd make sure I saw him enjoying the spectacle." Drake had to agree with her assessment; King was a supreme narcissist.

Romero seemed disappointed by her answer.

"Maybe someone who attended Fairstone's private viewing?" Jimmy put in. "They had access before the rest of us."

"Private viewing?" Romero asked. "When did this private showing occur?"

Drake answered. "This afternoon, once the installation was completed. Just an intimate group of about twenty, any of them could have had time to plan this."

"The devices were strictly amateur—easy to download instructions from the web and the components could be found at any Kmart." Romero shrugged. "I'm gonna hit the computer anyway, see if any of this fits a signature we've got on file."

"ATF as well?" Drake asked.

Romero shot him a look that said he didn't need to tell him how to do his job.

Chapter 7

It was almost three in the morning before Cassie, with Jimmy's help, was able to coax Drake away from the museum and back home to the apartment they shared on the top floor of his building in East Liberty. During that time, they'd reviewed recordings from dozens of security cameras, only to find that the crucial one had been blacked out during the time the incendiary devices were planted. Like the devices themselves, the camera had been circumvented by low-tech means: a dolly containing a large, draped sculpture had been parked in front of the camera for twelve minutes earlier that afternoon. Of course, there was now no trace of the sculpture or its paperwork.

The arson investigator, Romero, had also dissected Drake's case history, searching for someone who might have a grudge against Drake. There were a few names he and Jimmy came up with, disgruntled customers Jimmy called them, but a quick check confirmed they were all still incarcerated.

Jimmy still insisted on placing a protective detail outside Drake's building—something Drake usually would have balked at, but agreed to readily. Because of Cassie, she knew. Fine by her; the officers would be protecting him as much as her.

Drake's frustration and anger was broadcast via the rigid set of his shoulders as they climbed the stairs to their apartment. "You should get some rest." Cassie resorted to making small talk. "Your mom, and Nellie and Jacob, are stopping here for brunch before the rehearsal tomorrow."

He gave a grunt. "I don't understand this whole having the rehearsal party at Tessa's house when the wedding's going to be here. And why do you have to leave early just to try on your dress? It's my mom's—not like I haven't seen pictures of it."

With Christmas Eve on a Saturday and all their friends and Drake's relatives having the twenty-third off, Adeena, Cassie's best friend and maid of honor, had planned their rehearsal party for Friday afternoon at the house she shared with her Great Aunt Tessa.

"Because that's the way your mother wanted it. You're her only child and your family is also the only family I have left, and she's excited about me wearing her dress, so I expect you to indulge her and smile. A lot."

They reached the apartment door but he didn't unlock it, instead turned to scowl at her. "I'm not a child and this isn't self-pity."

"I know that. You're worried. That what happened tonight is only the beginning. That maybe we should cancel the wedding, tell everyone to stay home. That maybe we shouldn't stay here tonight and should just head out of town and hold up in a cheap motel in a town we don't even know the name of."

That cracked his facade. Not by much, the worry still leaked into his smile, but it was a start. "Am I that predictable?"

She stood on her tiptoes to kiss his nose. "Yes. Which is why I'll wait here while you clear the apartment and secure it."

"And everyone thinks I'm marrying you for your money." A joke since she had none. In fact, between the two of them pouring everything they had into the Liberty Center, if they did run away, they'd probably be sleeping in the back of his car.

He unlocked the door, cracked it open far enough to check the alarm panel and enter his code, then, leaving the lights off, entered with his gun drawn. She waited impatiently as Hennessey, her overweight tortoiseshell cat, meandered through the open door to whine about being left alone. Finally, Drake returned, snapping on the foyer light, and they all entered.

He took her coat and hung up his own as well, his

movements taut, still not relaxed despite being in the safety of their home. He'd never get any rest at this rate. Good thing Cassie knew a surefire way to relax them both.

He turned back to her, his expression revealing as much emotion as a blank slate. But she didn't need to see emotion on his face to know what was churning just beneath the surface. The storm-tossed indigo of his eyes did that for her, as did his knotted shoulder muscles. She led him to the bedroom, turning on only the shaded bedside lamp.

"I'm in no mood," he said, hands dug deep into his pocket, shoulders hunched. She ignored him, kicked off her shoes and lifted her skirt to slide out of her panties, letting them drop to the floor. She was now naked beneath the velvet folds of the dress and Drake knew it.

Still, he tried to turn away. "Cassie." He almost growled her name in protest as she moved to him. It was funny how he only used her first name when he was irritated with her.

She'd know she'd broken through to him when he reverted to his more familiar, intimate use of her surname. The way he said it, that one syllable, could send thrills roiling through her body. Sometimes she hated the way he could affect her—a single word or glance or touch could leave her helpless.

She raised her hands to his shoulders, playfully flicking the straps of his suspenders. Her smile was wicked as he moved his hands to cover hers, to try to stop her from proceeding.

Wrong move, she thought, leaning forward to nip his hand, letting her teeth sink into his flesh with enough force to distract any man.

"Damn it, Hart!"

Victory, she thought, sliding the suspenders from his shoulders even as he drew her to her tiptoes, his mouth devouring hers.

❧

DRAKE SQUEEZED HART'S shoulders, crushing the velvet of her gown in his sweaty palms. He yanked the cloth away, letting it slide down to hang in the crook of her arms, leaving her chest bare to him. As he bent to kiss her, he felt her intake of breath stealing his. Her hands slid between their bodies, fumbling with the buttons on his shirt. She made a small noise of frustration and yanked hard on the fabric, popping buttons in all directions.

He fisted one hand in her hair, unraveling the intricate braid, and tugged on it, pulling her head back so his mouth was free to roam her body. A sheen of sweat was all that separated them as she slid his shirt away from him. Then her fingers began to dance a tortuous tango down his spine until they found the sensitive spot at the small of his back, beneath his waistband. His hips arched in anticipation; he knew what would happen once she touched that spot just so. He was already aroused. He didn't believe she could coax any more from his body.

But, as usual, Hart surprised him. Her fingers drew away, teasing, taunting, before moving closer once more. Her leg skimmed up the back of his, drawing his hips to hers, layers of fabric still separating them below, creating a delicious friction.

Then her fingers touched that small area of skin that sent a jolt of electricity through every nerve ending. Drake caught his breath; pain and pleasure surged through him, exquisite and demanding in its urgency.

Hart raised her head, her mouth grazing his ear. "I want you, now," she commanded. He was only too willing to comply.

He gave her a gentle push onto the bed, the now rumbled and twisted folds of velvet still separating him from what he desired, what he needed. He knelt between her legs, grabbed both sides of her gown's hem and ripped the fabric upward. The tearing noise echoed his own desire and finally, she lay naked, open before him.

He didn't take the time to do more than slide his pants down before he joined her on the bed. She wrapped her legs around him and he was inside her, thrusting with an urgency that had been building all night long. Hart pulled him ever deeper and as he reared his head to give voice to the fury and passion that climaxed within him, he realized this was what he wanted to render in his art, this feeling of exhilaration, of awe over the power of two people joined together. Her face flushed with color, eyes wide as her mouth opened in her own primal scream of pleasure.

The animal who had taken *Steadfast* from him had won a shallow victory indeed. Drake looked upon Hart and knew this was the real prize, this power he and Hart shared, and he would do anything in the world to protect it.

And her.

CHAPTER 8

DRAKE WOKE A few hours later, his vision filled with the tableau he'd seen earlier at the gala: Hart with Adeena and Denise. The painting composed itself in his mind; he could imagine the layers of pigment, the swirl of the brushstrokes, how he would shape the light and perspective, bend them to suit his needs.

One day he'd recreate *Steadfast*—more for his own pleasure, to prove that animals didn't rule the world, not his world, anyway. But first he wanted to paint the three women—*Three Graces* he would call it.

Leaving Hart to sleep, he moved into his studio just as the sunrise streamed its pearlescent light through the eastern facing windows. His favorite time to sit and sketch, before the city was fully aroused, before he had to face the rigors of his own work day, while night-soaked dreamscapes and images remained fresh in mind. He draped the remnants of Hart's dress over an easel where the first rays of the sun caught the shimmer of light trapped in the folds of purple velvet.

He took his pad and, instead of charcoal, grabbed a pencil. These were only preliminary studies, a mapping out of the images he wanted, so vibrant in his mind but so difficult to translate onto paper and canvas.

He let his mind wander as he worked.

Steadfast had been about capturing and using light to convey the emotion of the piece. He'd experimented repeatedly until he'd developed a technique with pigments and dyes that allowed the canvas to absorb a fraction of the light and reflect the rest. It had been tedious and frustrating finding that right balance between light and light, the solid and the transparent, luminescent, but worth it in the end.

Grace would be more about shadow he realized as he looked down on his first sketch. Adeena so dark, Denise so fair, and Hart in the middle. As always, Hart would be the crux of the image.

He'd drawn her just as he'd seen her last night: that slightly crooked smile, those eyes that had seen too much to allow any moment of happiness to be disregarded, filled with knowledge that threatened to taint the joy.

Yet it didn't. And that was the battle, wasn't it? How to reveal the shadows that clung to Hart's life, darkness that would have long ago devoured a less sturdy soul, and balance them with the joy she brought to her life—and his.

Shadow and light. His fingers kept moving, playing. A tricky balance to find, to use flat pigments and canvas to express the emotions that fueled a soul.

But now that he knew what he wanted, half the battle was won. The rest was just endless experimentation, trial and error.

With *Steadfast*, he'd unveiled Hart's courage—which she would deny wholeheartedly, saying she was afraid of almost everything, but he knew better.

Drake looked once more on the face of the woman he loved and felt he had uncovered a new understanding of her. Balance was extremely important to her life. Just as it was for him. He was constantly striving, either as a cop or an artist, to create order out of chaos, to find a balance he could reproduce in his own life.

Adeena and Denise were studies in movement, laughter rippling through them. Hart was the center, moving, responding, full of raw emotion, yet also curiously still.

He was reminded of a film he'd seen in seventh grade social studies class. Whirling dervishes, their faces filled with a calm transfixion as they communed with God while their bodies embraced perpetual motion in a flawless, graceful dance of life. Which came first, the motion or the calm? He wondered and drew Hart's image once more, this time using a page to render her face alone.

Eye of a hurricane—the calm, serene center of the

storm created by raging winds circling around the edge. That was Hart. She had no need to search for balance or strive for it, she just was. It explained why her actions did indeed speak louder than words—they were created by primal forces instructing her in what needed to be done to maintain that precious balance.

The scratch of the pencil was the only sound in the room. Drake filled in shadows, balancing the light, but wasn't happy with the results. The pencil wouldn't do. He had the composition he wanted, but the rest of the image would be built by color and texture. Lots of metals—maybe even grind some gold or silver directly into some of the pigment? He looked at the rose blush of light shimmering from the folds of Hart's dress. No, not silver or gold. Copper.

He thought about seeing Hart work in the cacophony of the ER, watching her during a trauma resuscitation, or when she'd confronted violence. Somehow Hart always kept her equilibrium, knowing what action needed to be taken and doing it without hesitation.

Drake marveled at that. A man on a constant quest for stability in his life, he'd found a woman with a perfect sense of balance.

But the only way to stay centered was to acknowledge the chaos that swirled around her, constantly working to tear into the calm eye of the storm, devour it.

Those were the shadows. The price Hart paid for being Hart, the price Drake would pay for loving her.

He shook his head, banishing morbid thoughts into the brilliant rays of the rising sun, condemning them to a fiery death.

It did not always have to be that way—would not, not as long as the two of them were together.

CHAPTER 9

SINCE BOTH CASSIE and Drake enjoyed cooking, making brunch for his family was an enjoyable, well-choreographed dance as they moved around their small but well-equipped kitchen. She even saw him smile once or twice—real smiles, not "I'd rather be down at the station chasing the guy who dared burn my work of art," fakes. Whatever work he'd done in his studio this morning had refreshed his mood.

Maybe it was greedy of her, wanting her soon-to-be groom happy and relaxed before their wedding tomorrow night, but she didn't care. They'd both been through so much to make it here she refused to let anyone steal this moment from them.

She moved into the kitchen and finished making the

coffee while Drake's family—his mother, aunt, and uncle—gathered around the table, dissecting the press coverage of last night's events. Soon a tantalizing aroma filled the air. Drake might be the gourmet, but no one made coffee like Cassie. Gram Rosa had taught her how to turn ordinary beans into a thick, strong brew that tasted of ambrosia, not a bitter drop to be found.

She was silent as she walked around the table, filling cups, listening with a smile as Jacob and Nellie decried the *Tribune's* lack of standards.

"Their headline editor should be taken out and thrashed," Jacob said, pointing to the banner displayed on his iPad. "Terrorism strikes Fairstone unveiling," he read. "Garbage. Absolute sensationalistic garbage."

"But, Remy, the photos of the paintings—even though they're grainy—are stunning. Absolutely stunning," Drake's Aunt Nellie told him.

"I wish I'd been there," Muriel said, laying a proud hand on her son's arm. "All those people applauding your work, not even knowing who you were."

"They do now." Drake grimaced. Cassie filled his mug. His hand moved to light on her waist and she left a kiss on the top of his head before moving on.

"Still, I'm so proud of you, Remy."

Cassie returned the pot to the kitchen and leaned on the bar, watching the family—her family soon, she thought. It had been a very long time since she was a part of a family. It was exciting and scary at the same time. There were at least three conversations going on at the table, overlapping, weaving back and forth without missing a beat.

She started the frittata. Drake would graze all day, but life in the ER had taught Cassie to eat a full meal whenever she found time, and she was certain the others would want something more substantial than toast and jam.

As she beat eggs, she wondered at families—everyone had different names, different faces with their families. Drake was DJ—Drake Junior—to other cops, Remy to his family, Drake to everyone else—but he'd once told Cassie that he preferred Mickey, the same name his father had gone by. So, even though he was Drake to her most of the time, she'd begun to call him Mickey when they were most intimate, when emotions were at their strongest. Four names but one man.

She thought at that. His aunt, Eleanor Steadman, was Nellie to friends and family, despite the fact that she was a Pulitzer prize-winning investigative journalist under her maiden name: Eleanor DeAngelo. And Cassie had noted that when they spoke of work, Nellie called her husband, Jacob, by his surname, Steadman—a habit from their days on the newspaper together, she guessed.

Even Cassie had her share of nicknames. As a child the only people who called her Cassandra were the nuns or Gram Rosa when she was in trouble—which was so often that she'd grown to despise the sound of her full name.

Friends who knew her when she was a kid called her Cassie. As an adult, most people used her surname, Hart. She'd grown to like the strong sound of the single syllable. It evoked confidence, a sense of competence. Except when Drake used it—then the name seemed to connote the vital organ. She smiled as she thought of the way Drake could make that single syllable sound powerful, thrilling, knowing that he meant her when he said it.

Then there was her first husband, Richard's dreaded nickname for her, Ella, short for Cinderella.

She whipped the eggs without mercy. Maybe some nicknames were best forgotten.

AFTER BRUNCH, DRAKE'S family gleefully kidnapped Cassie, Muriel chattering away about how she couldn't wait to see Cassie in her wedding dress. They drove to Adeena's house in Bloomfield where she lived with her Great Aunt Tessa, who had been Cassie's Gram Rosa's best friend.

Despite being a low-budget, homegrown affair, the entire wedding was like that—friends and family coming together to celebrate Cassie and Drake's happiness.

Adeena and Tessa hosted the rehearsal party, scheduled early enough in the day so that all the kids who were participating could enjoy it. The priest presiding over their non-traditional ceremony was retired, but had also officiated Adeena and Cassie's first communions and confirmations and had been a close friend of Tessa and Rosa.

Cassie thought he'd never agree to perform the ceremony since Drake wasn't Catholic and she hadn't been to Mass in years, but apparently Father Serrano had grown more liberal as the years passed. Or Tessa had twisted his arm. Despite being blind and suffering from diabetes, she was just as imposing as Gram Rosa, able to bend almost anyone to her will.

When they arrived at Tessa's house, Andy Greally was already there, setting up the food for the party. He'd been Drake's first partner on the police force and, now that he was retired, ran a bar where he enjoyed practicing his culinary skills. Denise Dolan was also there, blowing up balloons that her twins, Bridget and Colton, were having fun floating around the room.

"Where's Jimmy?" Cassie asked after greeting Tessa, who sat like a queen overseeing things from her chair at the head of the dining room table.

Denise smiled. "He and Drake are working on a surprise for you."

"Oh no. Drake and I agreed, no gifts. We're putting all our money into the Liberty Center."

"Hah, you just want me to tell you what it is. Not going to work," she replied in a singsong.

Adeena hustled Cassie up the steps to her bedroom where the box that held Muriel's dress waited. They'd been best friends since second grade and the room hadn't changed much over the years. The walls had gone from pink to purple to a warm yellow and the decor was no longer magazine cutouts of Hollywood stars, but the furniture was the same maple dresser and double bed that they'd jumped on as girls.

"I can't believe this is actually happening," Adeena gushed. "You're getting married. And on Christmas Eve. It's just so romantic." She flopped on to the bed that had shared years of their giggles, secrets, and adolescent angst.

Cassie looked down at her friend's smiling face. "I can't believe it either," she confessed, sinking to the edge of the bed, the dress box propped across her legs.

"Oh no, I know that look—" Adeena sat up abruptly. "You're not having second thoughts are you? Not about Drake?"

Cassie was silent. Not about Drake. About her. She'd failed so spectacularly at her first marriage, how could she risk a second? When she'd seen all those people downstairs—people here to wish her and Drake happiness, to share in their joy, she realized how many people would be hurt—that she would hurt—if she failed again.

"Drake's not Richard," Adeena went on, pulling Cassie's hair back from her face so Cassie couldn't hide behind it. "And you're not the same person either. You've been given a second chance. You can't just turn your back on what you and Drake have."

Adeena combed her fingers through Cassie's hair, separating the strands and weaving them into intricate braids just as she used to do when they were twelve. "I wish I could find someone like him." She sighed wistfully and paraphrased their catch phrase from senior high. "But a good man is hard to find."

Cassie smiled, her fears receding as childhood memories returned. "And a hard man—"

"Is good to find," they finished together.

"It was so unfair," Cassie went on as Adeena completed her braiding. "In high school, I was the one always getting into trouble, who everyone assumed was the 'bad' girl, while you were doing half the basketball team!"

"Hey a girl's got to go with her talents. Mine just happen to be communication and personal relationship skills," Adeena replied archly.

"That's not what the graffiti in the girls' room said."

"Girls can be so petty when they're jealous." She sat back and admired her work. "Let's see how that dress looks."

Cassie left the bed and carefully opened the box. Folds of white silk spilled over the tissue paper they were wrapped in. She wiped her hands on her jeans and gingerly pulled the dress out.

"It's gorgeous." Adeena slid a finger over the freshwater pearls sewn to the bodice. "Did Muriel really make this herself?"

"Drake said her mother helped her. Muriel always wanted to be a fashion designer but left school and took a job at the ad agency after she got married." Cassie held the dress against her body, swirling around and feeling faintly like Cinderella.

"Go ahead, put it on."

Cassie hesitated. The dress was the most beautiful thing she'd ever been given. But what was even more valuable was the thought and generosity that had come with the gift. Muriel's acceptance and approval was as dear to Cassie as the wedding gown.

Finally, she slid out of her shoes and clothes and Adeena helped her to lift the gown down over her head. The bodice was formfitting with tiny triangles over the shoulders that dropped down over her upper arms. Otherwise, the gown was sleeveless, the skirt billowing out from under a yoked waist, full but not puffy, with no need for crinolines or flounces, just a simple underskirt for modesty. Tear drops of pearls hung from the shoulders, the edge of the bodice and along the tea-length hem, creating movement that caught the eye, drawing it down the length of the dress. Cassie pirouetted in front of Adeena's full-length mirror, one hand caught to the bare skin above the neckline, unable to believe the woman in the mirror could be her.

Adeena clapped her hands as she circled around, admiring the dress from every angle. "It's perfect."

"Hey, you girls!" Tessa's voice rang like a church bell. "What's taking so long?"

Cassie and Adeena turned to each other, giggling like girls caught playing with forbidden make up and nail polish. "Coming!" they called out in unison.

Adeena turned to Cassie and wrapped her arms around her friend. "I'm so happy for you," she whispered.

Adeena went down the steps first, leaving Cassie to make an entrance. Cassie could hear voices, happy, laughing voices, drifting up from the living room. She picked out Andy Greally's guffaw mixing with Ed Castro's more nasal laugh; Nellie's precise, cultured voice mingled with Tammy Washington's and Denise Dolan's Pittsburghese. Denise's twins, Bridget and Colton, were concocting a story about rescue heroes and spacemen with Antwan, Tammy's little boy. Father Serrano's low murmur echoed up the stairwell as he and Jacob debated religious tenets.

All these people here for her. Cassie shook her head as she gripped the banister. She'd always thought of herself as a loner. When Rosa died, she'd lost the last of her family. Then Richard had isolated her from anyone who could have saved her. So she had saved herself and avoided future emotional entanglements. Or so she thought. The truth of the number of people she'd accidentally allowed into her life, her heart, was frightening.

As Cassie walked barefoot down the stairs into Tessa's living room, the conversation stopped and all heads turned to her. Even the children's squeals quieted. She reached the bottom step and three-year-old Antwan Washington ran up to her, his mouth open wide in surprise.

"Dr. Cass, you're a fairy princess!" he exclaimed,

breaking the silence that had settled over the room.

Bridget raced to take Cassie's hand. "Me too, I'm a princess too!" She and Antwan, followed by her brother, tugged Cassie off the steps and into the crowd of people. Soon Cassie found herself smothered in hugs and kisses and well wishes as the living room swirled with activity. There were presents piled on the coffee table, most of the ones from the men bearing the distinctive wrapping paper of a well-known lingerie chain. Even the kids had gotten into the act, Cassie saw as she noted two presents wrapped with paper lovingly colored with crayon, her name printed in painstaking letters.

"You kids come get into your seats," Tessa commanded, the blind woman effortlessly herding the perpetual motion of the three children to the dining room table. "No fingers on that wedding dress, but you can have some apple pie while we wait for Drake."

The doorbell rang as Cassie was starting up the stairs to change out of the dress. She was still blinking back tears of joy and needed a few moments privacy.

"I've got it," Cassie said, moving to open the door. She glanced through the leaded glass of the sidelight. It was a man. The man from last night at the gallery, the one who'd frightened her. He'd mentioned Drake, spoke as if they knew each other—had Drake invited him?

She opened the door. Then she saw the two men with him. The two men with guns.

CHAPTER 10

NICKOLAI KASANOV MOTIONED to the men on either side of him to hold their positions out of sight. The door opened, and to his delight, Rosa Costello's granddaughter answered it herself. He smiled his most charming smile, showing gleaming teeth polished to perfection. It was a smile that those who knew him best dreaded, with good reason.

"Can I help you?" she asked, her face flushing as his gaze moved down the formfitting wedding dress and then back up to rest on her face. She was the image of Rosa Costello. Exactly as his father had described the witch. Eyes dark as coal, promising as much heat, hair a riot of thick curls to tempt and torment a man, ivory skin as transparent as alabaster, exotic cheekbones of a houri.

"I am Nickolai Kasanov," he said, injecting a note of

pleasant formality into his voice. "I have come to congratulate the bride-to-be."

Her face filled with confusion as his men stepped into the doorway, filling it with their bulk, Hart trapped between them. No, not confusion, he noted. Indecision. Was she really considering fighting? How precious.

Nickolai nodded to his men and each of them took one of Hart's arms, propelling her with them inside the house before she could protest. Nickolai followed, closing the door behind him.

"Everyone will please remain calm," he said. His companions raised their guns. One aimed his at Hart, dodging a kick from her bare foot. But what stopped her from resisting further was when the second aimed at the two men who rushed forward. Nickolai recognized them from his reconnaissance: Andrew Greally, Drake's former partner, and Edward Castro, a doctor who worked with Hart. They would be the only two who would pose any risk; Jacob Steadman was too old and too smart to rush into a fight with such overwhelming odds and the priest would of course be useless.

"What do you want?" Hart ignored the men with the guns and turned to face Nickolai.

God, she had spirit, gall. Questioning him, challenging him? Nickolai took a step forward, his eyes locked on Hart's, his face never changing, not telegraphing the blow he was about to strike.

His hand flew out and the sound of the slap rang

through the silent room. Hart's head flew back, her eyes widened in surprise, and she staggered, dropping to her knees. His smile widened as women's voices hushed a child's cry in the next room. He grabbed her hair and yanked her head back to meet his gaze. Blood trickled from her nose, splashing in bright red petals on the white silk gown.

"You, Dr. Hart. I want you."

Her eyes flared with rebellion. She had no idea who she was dealing with or she would have never allowed him to see that. Many of his comrades shied away from dealing with women as hostages—they were too strong, too difficult to breakdown and control. Too unpredictable.

Which made them a delightful challenge in Nickolai's view. Because once he found their weak spot, their final destruction was all the more spectacular.

The sounds of running feet distracted him and tiny hands pummeled him from behind. "Don't do that!" a boy's voice cried out. Nickolai turned and grabbed both of the boy's hands in one of his. "Don't you hurt her! She's my friend." The boy was sobbing, still struggling to protect Hart.

A tall blonde crossed into the room. Nickolai saw her glance dart from a girl the same age as the boy and back to the boy. Ah, the Dolan twins and their mother—such fascinating possibilities. One of the men, Greally, the barkeep with the florid complexion, shook his head at her and she froze.

"Let him go," Hart said.

Nickolai squatted, twisting the squirming child onto his knee, his free hand tousling his hair. He ignored the fury in Hart's eyes and bent his head close to the boy's.

"She's your friend?" he said softly. The boy stopped and sniffed hard.

"Please." Hart was pleading now. Nickolai liked that. "I'll do anything you want—"

Still he ignored her. "What's your name?"

The boy sniffed again then answered. "Colton Dolan."

Nickolai released the boy's hands and turned him to face him. "You're a very brave boy, Colton Dolan," he said in a grave voice. He held out his hand. "I'm Nickolai Kasanov."

The boy took the hand and shook it in a parody of adult comradeship. "Now, Colton," Nickolai continued, his gaze never leaving the boy's, his voice low and hypnotic, "would you rather come with Dr. Hart and me, ride in a big car and go on an adventure? Or do you want to go back to your sister and mother and finish your pie?"

Nickolai heard the mother's stifled sob behind him. Colton shifted his weight in indecision.

"Go back to your mother and Bridget," Hart told Colton. "You have to take care of them until your father gets here."

Colton yanked his gaze from Nickolai and turned to Hart. "But who's gonna take care of you, Cassie?" he asked, his voice filled with concern.

Nickolai looked on in admiration as Hart smiled at the boy. "I can take care of myself. You know that."

Colton nodded gravely. He smiled, showing a missing front tooth. "Dad says you're not afraid of anything."

"That's right. So I want you to walk back to your chair and stay close to your mom and sister until your father comes. Can you do that?" He nodded. "Promise?"

"Cross my heart and hope to—" She pulled him close, muffling his words in her embrace, kissing the top of his head. Her eyes locked with Nickolai's and she released the boy, pushing him away from Nickolai and back toward the dining room.

"Nicely done," Nickolai said. He stood and turned to the crowd, ignoring Hart, showing her that she held no threat to him. "But I still need a hostage," he announced.

The adults all looked up at that, the two mothers drawing close to their children, the blind woman reaching a hand out for her great niece. She was a possibility; Nickolai hated old, blind women. Everyone automatically gave them respect for doing nothing more than surviving on the charity and benevolence of others. Worthless waste of resources. If he had his way, every blind woman, every old beggar, everyone who survived by leeching off another's goodwill, would be shot.

His eyes moved to the stooped man in the cassock. That went doubly for priests and nuns—not only did they make their living from the people's generosity, they encouraged false hope and a promise of paradise that was a delusion.

But this was not the time or place to indulge in philosophy. No, he needed the person who would allow him to control both Hart and Drake. His eyes lit on a dark-haired woman who stared at him with almost as much revulsion as Hart had. Except her eyes also held more than a trace of fear. Nickolai smiled. He knew this woman.

"Which one of you is Muriel Drake?" he asked.

The tall, dark-haired woman moved forward immediately, taking a step in front of a smaller woman with blue eyes and the same dark hair. "I am," she said in a level voice, ignoring the hand of the gray-haired man who reached out to restrain her.

"No, that won't do, Mrs. Steadman," Nickolai chided. "Please don't mistake me for a fool—you should know me better than that. But it is nice to finally meet you." He moved forward to take her cold hand in his and lift it to his lips. "Did you get the present I sent you?" he murmured, enjoying the look of terror that filled her eyes.

He felt her hand tremble in his as she tried to jerk free. He held her in place for a moment then released her. She stumbled backward and he reached beside her to draw out the woman she'd tried to shield. Muriel Drake shared her son's eyes and dark hair but she was small boned, even shorter than Hart.

"Mrs. Drake, I'm so pleased to make your acquaintance. I know your family is anticipating a wedding tomorrow night. If you and Dr. Hart would accompany me,

I'll do everything I can to have you back in time." He drew her forward, away from the crowd as if inviting her onto the dance floor.

As they neared the door, he turned around, making eye contact with each of the adults in turn. "I'm certain you all understand the consequences to everyone involved if we are followed or detained in anyway. Tell Detective Drake that he may want to stay close to his phone. I'll be calling soon."

Chapter 11

CASSIE ALLOWED HERSELF to be led from the house, watching helpless as Kasanov's thugs escorted Muriel to a Lincoln Town Car parked at the curb and shoved her inside.

A second, identical car pulled up behind it. Kasanov opened the rear door for Cassie. She tensed, thinking this might be her best opportunity to escape, knowing the others inside the house would be watching for a chance to save the situation, waiting on her cue.

"Please, Dr. Hart, don't underestimate me like Mrs. Steadman did. I've read all about your tendency for heroics," Kasanov said calmly, reaching into his pocket. Instead of the gun Cassie expected, he pulled out a handheld radio. "My men are listening—anything goes wrong and Mrs. Drake will be killed."

Cassie resisted the urge to spit in his face—adolescent antics would do nothing to improve the situation. But it would have made her feel better, given her some brief sense of control. Not to mention the satisfaction of wiping that greasy smile from his face.

Kasanov seemed disappointed by her docility as she climbed into the car, pulling the folds of the wedding dress in with her.

"I've lived this long by learning not to believe everything I hear," he told her once he'd joined her in the back seat. "But also by not underestimating anyone I deal with. You can rest assured that if it had suited my purposes, I would have left no witnesses, would have snapped that boy's neck if only to prove to you who is in control here."

Cassie was silent as he lounged against the corner, not bothering with a seat belt. He had wanted to leave witnesses. Why? A message for Drake could have been just as easily sent with dead bodies. She had a suspicion that it was some form of misdirection, but she couldn't see how. Kasanov hadn't even bothered with the comic book formula of telling them not to call the police—which would be the first thing Andy would do.

She wasn't surprised then when they pulled into a parking garage and she was hustled into a second vehicle, a light gray Dodge Caravan, complete with a "Baby on Board" bumper sticker. The car Muriel was in was nowhere to be seen. How far was his radio's range? she wondered.

"What do you want?" she finally asked as they drove off in the van, hidden from traffic behind tinted windows.

"Tell me about your grandmother." He surprised her. "Tell me about what she did during the war."

Cassie frowned. "Why do you care about Rosa? What does she have to do with this?"

"Rosa Costello stole everything from me—my father, our family pride, my legacy. It's because of Rosa Costello that I am who I am." He smiled at this, the wide grin of a predator. Cassie felt a chill enter the pit of her stomach.

"No matter what happens here you can blame it on your beloved grandmother—Rosa Costello, the bitch." He spat out the last, a glob of saliva splattering the skirt of Muriel's dress.

Cassie shifted on the bench seat, protectively pulling the fabric closer to her. Kasanov's face clouded in fury and he grabbed her, his hand bunching in the folds of silk, yanking her closer to him, ignoring the ripping noise as the skirt caught on the seat buckle.

"Don't make me beat it out of you," he snarled, all pretenses at civilization shattered. "As much as I would love to. Because, for the short time, anyway, I need you alive. And if you die, so does Drake's mother—" He pinched her cheeks in his hands, squeezing her face, forcing her to look at him, to see truth of his threats.

Finally, he released her. She crumbled against the seat back, her chest heaving as she fought for air.

Kasanov crossed his legs, shaking out the crease in his

pants leg. "Now. Tell me about your grandparents," he commanded. "Where did they hide the treasure?"

That's when Cassie's courage faltered. Because in all of her grandparents' tales of their adventures during the war, neither had ever mentioned any kind of treasure.

"I don't know what you're talking about."

His slap came like lightning. For a man in his sixties, he had great reflexes. Cassie's cheek burned but she didn't touch it; instead, she simply stared at him. He was obviously smart, able to lead men, successful...but if he thought Rosa and Padraic had access to some hidden treasure, then he was also completely mad.

"Tell me where the gold is," he repeated. "I know they got it out of France—their escape cost my grandfather his life."

She shook her head. Then remembered. It wasn't a treasure, not by any definition, but..."Her perina. Rosa kept the gold in her perina."

A perina was a crazy quilt, a patchwork pieced together by generations of the women in Rosa's kumpania, each sewing small treasures beneath the fabric to guard against bad times.

Rosa had used her perina for more than a portable treasure chest. After her kumpania had been betrayed and the Nazis captured Rosa, they'd sent her to a prison farm. She'd ground manure and grass seed into the fabric of her perina and then used it as camouflage to help her escape.

Decades later, that same perina had saved Cassie's

life when her house was set on fire. Those ragged bits of fabric, sewn with love, were worth more to her than any treasure.

Kasanov obviously didn't see it that way. He glared at her. "I'm trying to decide if you're a fool or just ignorant. If you're playing with me, it's Drake's mother who will suffer."

"No," Cassie said. "That's the only gold I know anything about. Rosa and Padraic never had any money—they lived on a farm, could barely pay the bills. You must be mistaken."

"I am not mistaken," he told her in a slow, deadly voice. But then he paused and considered. "And I have no patience for liars." He raised the radio, gave a command in a language Cassie didn't understand. Then he held the radio up to her. "Listen."

A woman's screams pierced the air, drilling into Cassie.

Muriel.

"Stop, please. I'll do anything you want."

"Tell me where the gold is."

Muriel kept screaming, barely pausing long enough to breathe.

"I told you, I don't know. Rosa never talked about her past. I can't tell you what I don't know!"

Chapter 12

Drake spent the morning transforming the rooftop garden into a winter dreamland. Jimmy helped him transport warming lights and braziers, chairs for all the guests, canopies with clear plastic roofs to keep out the cold and let in the stars, and pots of Hart's favorite roses in full bloom despite the fact that it was December twenty-third.

Hart deserved magic, so he'd been happy to arrange it for her with the help of a local florist whose son had been falsely accused of murder until Drake and Jimmy found the real killer.

"She's going to love it," Jimmy assured him as they looked upon their handiwork. "But you're setting the bar high for the rest of us. Denise is going to expect something just as spectacular come our next anniversary." He glanced at his dirt-smeared work clothes. "We'd better get cleaned up or Tessa won't let us in her house."

They returned to Drake's apartment where Jimmy used the guest bath while Drake grabbed a quick shower and changed into jeans and a button-down shirt. He sat on the bed, one shoe in his hand, feeling as dazed as a man moving through a dream, the heat of the shower and pleasant ache from the morning's exertion adding to the illusion. As he smoothed a wrinkle from Rosa's quilt, a generations-old collection of faded and worn fabric, he realized he had everything he'd ever wanted from life.

In the past, the thought would have been terrifying. Having everything meant you could just as easily lose everything. But not now.

Now it brought a warm contentment. No pre-wedding jitters, no second thoughts. He'd gotten it right. What he had with Hart was true, more real than anything he'd ever experienced. He imagined her walking across the rooftop garden tomorrow night, a thousand lights competing with the stars above, and she'd outshine them all. Imagined the expression on her face, that smile when their gazes met—the smile he'd die for.

After everything they'd been through, they'd more than earned their fairy tale ending. He was so very proud he could give it to her.

A sharp knock on the door interrupted his fantasy. He hastily finished tying his shoe and stood. Jimmy opened the door without waiting. "We gotta go."

Drake immediately came to full alert. Jimmy's tone, filled with worry and urgency, sent all his hopes and dreams crumbling into ashes.

"What happened?"

THE VAN DROVE for a few more minutes, taking what felt like random turns, until the driver said something to Kasanov in a foreign language. It sounded a bit like Rosa's Romani, but Cassie only knew a few words of the native gypsy tongue, so wasn't sure.

Then they came to a stop. The driver opened the door beside Cassie and yanked her out, twisting her arm behind her and placing her in a wristlock that sent pain jolting down her arm. Kasanov joined them. This time they were inside an abandoned Quonset hut. A hanger? Cassie wondered, panic edging past her defenses. If he took her onto a plane, there was no way Drake could follow.

They were parked beside a black Ford Focus—the kind of car no one would look twice at or remember once it passed.

Kasanov opened the trunk and gestured to it. "Get in, Dr. Hart," he told her with a smile.

Cassie had the sudden feeling that Kasanov knew about her history of claustrophobia and panic attacks. She hadn't had any problems in months; thanks to Drake, she could even ride in an elevator now.

It was an oft-used technique with prisoners of war: first divide, then disorient, and finally conquer. That knowledge was no help as the familiar whirlpool of panic began to suck her in, stealing her breath, squeezing her chest, strangling her heart. The gaping maw of the car trunk shrank in her vision until it appeared as a suffocating small tomb. No, she couldn't do it. If she got inside there, she would die.

Cassie fought for control, digging her fingers into her palms until the bite of nails into flesh gave her something to focus on other than the terror that threatened to devour her.

Kasanov jerked her arm, pulling her closer to the dark void. She pulled away and he slapped her.

"I said, get inside." He reached for the two-way radio. "Would you like to hear Mrs. Drake scream again?"

"No, don't!" Cassie pushed against the edge of the trunk. Kasanov nodded to his driver who grabbed her arm and twisted it behind her back once more. He slid a pair of plastic zip ties over both wrists, pulling them so tight she felt the edges bite into her flesh.

"Give me the radio," she bargained. "So I know Muriel is still alive." A voice in the darkness, maybe she could survive if she could talk to Muriel.

"If I wanted her dead, she'd be dead," Kasanov said flatly.

The driver bent and cuffed her ankles with another set of zip ties, lifted her off her feet, and shoved her into the confined space. Cassie resisted, bucking her body, blocking the lid from being closed.

"I don't have all day." Kasanov raised the radio to his lips.

Swallowing a whimper, Cassie lowered herself the remainder of the way into the trunk before he could tell his comrades to hurt Muriel again. He grinned down at her, her last sight before the roof slammed shut.

If I die, he'll kill Muriel too. She fought for breath. The space stunk of gasoline, rubber, and spoiled meat as if some small furry creature had crawled in here to die. Guess that meant she wasn't alone, Cassie thought as hysteria threatened to overwhelm her defenses.

The car started and they lurched forward. Her body, already contorted in a painful position, was now slammed and bounced against hard surfaces as they traveled. A surge of nausea rose in Cassie's stomach and she clamped her jaw shut, swallowing the bile. Her hands and feet grew numb while painful stabs of muscle cramps shot through the rest of her body.

She almost didn't notice the pain; it was the least of her worries as panic overtook her.

Dead, she was dead. There was nothing she could do, couldn't breathe, her heart pounding so hard it was going to leap from her chest, couldn't even swallow, was going to gag—it didn't matter how, she was dying, going, gone.

She tried to fight—the battle for her mind more terrifying than her struggle with Kasanov. You've faced killers before, seen evil and beaten it; don't give up, a small voice tried to pierce the darkness that had enveloped her.

A voice that sounded like Drake's.

He'd always been there when she was at her most hopeless, always given her the strength she needed to overcome. Not now. Now she was alone.

She couldn't do it alone. The sobs echoed through the trunk as Cassie's spirit broke. She began to scream, to bang, pound on the walls with the frenzy of a madwoman. The only response when she finally quieted, head and knees bruised, throat raw, slumped in exhaustion, was the sound of laughter coming from the man in the rear seat.

Laughing as she died.

She had no more tears but cried just the same, certain each breath was her last. She curled up into the fetal position, whimpering, broken as darkness overtook her.

Then warm arms encircled her, snugging her into their embrace. She felt Drake's breath on her neck as he whispered in her ear, the steady comfort of his heartbeat against her back, his hands clasping hers tight, pouring his strength into her body.

She strained to hear his words but it was as if he were too far away. She tried to quiet her breathing, and finally the rushing in her brain subsided so that she could hear his gentle whisper.

"I'm here," he was saying. "I'll always be here." And he moved one of his hands to rest over her heart.

As their heartbeat and breathing synchronized, Cassie

allowed herself to fall into an exhausted stupor, cradled within the safety of Drake's arms.

CHAPTER 13

DRAKE INSISTED ON driving while Jimmy worked the phone and scanned any intersections they blasted through. Normally, the drive to Tessa's home in Bloomfield took twelve minutes, fifteen if the lights went against you; today, Drake ignored the lights and made it in half that time.

Racing down Penn Avenue, Jimmy calling "clear," and warning against traffic as Drake steered, was just like the old days when Drake was a rookie and Andy Greally was his training officer. But Drake didn't have time or energy to reminisce, all he could think about were Hart and his mother.

Thankfully Andy had been there, at the house. Drake was certain that was why there hadn't been bloodshed—Andy wouldn't have let the civilians panic. As soon as

Jimmy made sure everything was being done to mobilize the city's resources to find the kidnappers, he got Andy back on the line.

"Who the hell is this Kasanov?" Drake shouted into Jimmy's phone.

"Never heard of him, but your aunt has. Said she ran into him back when she was a reporter in Cleveland. Ran some mob outfit."

"Russian?" Not that it mattered, but if they knew Kasanov's associates, they might get some leverage. Drake spun the wheel and they screeched onto Tessa's street, already crowded with patrol cars. He skidded to a stop, double-parking beside Jimmy's wife's van.

Jimmy leapt from the Mustang, yelling for Denise and the kids, flashing his badge at the patrolman guarding the scene. As Bridget and Colton bounded from the house, leaping into Jimmy's arms, Drake slowed his steps. There was no one here for him to greet, no need for him to rush. The realization hit him like a sucker punch, knocking out all his wind until his knees wobbled. He clutched the thin iron handrail beside the steps leading up to Tessa's porch.

Hart was gone. His mother was gone. He stood there, the whirlwind of activity blurring around him. Inside, he felt emptied, a vacuum that had stolen everything: fear, anger, hope. Nothing left but a frozen, black void.

He inhaled; the air was warm for this late in December, at least fifty—no snow this year. The thoughts jumbled like pieces of a puzzle thrown into the air. Mixed in were images of *Steadfast* burning last night—only now it wasn't the painting he saw in flames, but Hart's face.

That she knew he was coming for her was the most comforting thought he could conjure. He couldn't let her down, her or his mother. Flimsy strands of desperation, but they were enough to guide him forward, one step at a time.

A patrolman opened the door for him, not even asking to see his ID. Jacob and Nellie rushed to his side, Nellie embracing him with a hug, Jacob standing back, observing—their usual partnership; reporter diving into the fray, editor reining her in when need be.

"They'll be fine," Nellie said between her own tears. "We called the police right away. There's no reason for him to hurt either one of them."

Drake gently disengaged her arms from his body. "What happened?"

Jacob stepped forward. "I got most of it on video—they didn't even ask us for our cell phones or anything. Like they didn't care what evidence they left behind."

Jimmy and Andy joined them as Jacob pulled out his phone. Drake realized they were the only detectives on scene—the patrolmen were more concerned with securing the scene and starting the manhunt than reviewing evidence.

Denise asked Adeena to take the kids upstairs with Tessa then she joined them as they watched Jacob's video. It started with Hart's arrival, followed by Adeena tugging her up the steps, a scene of the priest surrounded by the children, finally Hart descending the steps dressed in a wedding gown.

"You can't see that, it's bad—" Denise's hand went to her mouth before she could finish. "Sorry," she said, reaching a hand to squeeze Drake's shoulder.

Then the doorbell rang and everything changed. The two heavies with Kasanov; Hart at his feet, her face bloody, his hand twisting her hair; Kasanov with Colton on his knee, his eyes locked with Hart's; Hart pulling the boy from Kasanov; Muriel and Kasanov in the center of the room; Hart and Kasanov leaving with Muriel.

"That's Kasanov? He was at the Fairstone," Drake said. "He was there when they burned *Steadfast*."

Drake rewound the video and watched it again. He didn't care about the last part—seeing that once was more than enough. Instead, he lingered on the beginning, the part with his mother and Hart laughing and happy, whole and alive. Those images he carved into his heart.

"Who the hell is this guy?" Jimmy asked. "And what's he want with Hart and Muriel?"

"He's an Eastern European mobster," Nellie answered Jimmy. "I tried to do a story on him several years ago—one of the people who spoke to me was named Russo. The story died after I couldn't get anyone else to confirm what Russo told me, and a few days later, I received a package with a note from Kasanov." She cringed and Drake knew where this was going. "It was a human tongue—I gave it to the FBI in Cleveland. They confirmed it as Russo's and said it had been removed while he was alive. He's never been seen again."

Jacob wrapped an arm around her, but that didn't stop her trembling.

"Maybe he's using Hart to get to you?" Andy asked Drake.

"Why?" Drake clutched the phone, frozen on Hart's smiling face as she and Muriel hugged. "I have nothing to do with Kasanov—if he's with the mob, he's a federal problem, not local. I never even heard of the man before today. Why target Hart or me?"

Drake's questions went unanswered. The knot of despair tightened in his gut but he refused to give up hope.

They were alive—they had to be.

⁕

ONCE CASSIE FORCED her panic away, the ride became surreal. Kasanov's men had prepared the trunk, bolting sheets of metal over the vulnerable spots like the tail lights and electrical connections as well as barricading the space in front of the back seat with a length of plywood, giving her no escape route and no light. The space was so small that no matter how she twisted her body she ended up folded, her weight pressed on the delicate joints of her wrists and ankles. Once they became numb, any new movement sent electrical jolts of pain through her—bad enough that the car's erratic bumps and turns did that, so she gave up trying to reposition herself and simply focused on being... elsewhere.

Deep, calming breaths, forcing her muscles to relax, clearing her mind...at first she heard Drake's voice, reassuring her that he was coming for her, that everything would be all right. Then another voice, equally strong and comforting, came through: her grandfather's.

After her mom died, Cassie had spent a lot of her childhood with Padraic and Rosa on their farm in St. Augustine. Cassie loved both her grandparents deeply, but Rosa with her gypsy curses and impossible standards was too formidable for a little girl to approach.

Paddy never minded her tagging along with him, called her his shadow, never tiring of her endless questions or begging for stories from the war he and Rosa had fought. A natural storyteller, he was delighted to oblige, filling their hours of chores with tales that cemented Rosa's image as larger-than-life, often downplaying his own role in events. But Cassie knew better—her grandfather was a hero.

She treasured every moment spent with him; he was her closest friend, and the one person she could trust with her feelings. It wasn't until years after he was gone that she realized he must have felt the same about her, entrusting her with the truth of what he and Rosa had done, things she never fully understood until she was older and wiser.

As much as she loved her father and worshiped her grandmother, it was Paddy she adored without reservation. His strong, hairy arms, thick as small tree trunks; his large, calloused hands; the scent of cherry pipe tobacco that followed him everywhere; the lilting Irish accent and occasional lapse into Gaelic; his easy grin and the laugh that would rumble out of him like a volcano erupting. His was a presence solid, warm, comforting, and loving.

"Tell me a story," she'd beg, cuddling into his embrace. He'd already told her how he and Rosa met during the war. In November of 1940, his ship had been torpedoed by U-boats off the coast of France, but Rosa and her group of Maquis had rescued Paddy. "Tell me about how you and Rosa saved your crew."

Paddy puffed on his pipe, and then nodded his agreement. "It all started with a root cellar and a bushel of turnips."

CHAPTER 14

IN HER MIND, Cassie was safe and sound at Paddy and Rosa's farm, far away from the pitch-black pain of the endless car ride to an unknown fate.

"I quickly realized I'd been rescued by a crazy woman." Padraic continued his story. "Just as fast realized she was the leader of this crew of French brigands who seemed as like to toss us back to the mercy of the storm as drag us onto dry land once they realized we were none of us officers."

The scent of cherry pipe tobacco softened his words. "Course, I had a secret weapon. I was the radio operator and the officers had taught me German and a bit of French, so I could report anything I heard. Turns out languages came as easy to me as did mimicking old Father O'Brien's

Latin or the nuns' mincing tirades. One thing I've always been good at—be it a birdcall or a whiff of a tune, if I hear it once, I can repeat it. Good thing, too. That gift of gab and playacting saved our lives more than once.

"Rosa didn't care we weren't officers, but her men complained that the Brits only paid them to rescue officers. She quickly had them in hand with only a word or two I didn't understand, some language not German nor French, but the men—all of them ages older than her, mind you, I didn't learn it until later, but she was barely seventeen at the time, already fighting the Nazis years longer than any army, already blood on her hands—the men jerked their heads up at those words, searching the storm clouds as if waiting for lightning to strike, and bent their backs to their oars, bringing us into shore."

"I'll bet she cursed them," young Cassie whispered into her grandfather's shoulder. She knew how the men felt— Rosa could turn her bones to jelly with just a stern look, didn't need to resort to using any of her Romani curses.

"There was one thing they kept repeating. *La tempête.* The storm, I thought they meant. Figured out the truth later that night after we'd dragged the boats ashore and hid them. Nine of my mates had been saved by Rosa's crew, another twenty-two by her other boats. No officers, but one of Rosa's men who'd stayed on shore, monitoring the radio, said the Vichy had taken seven British officers prisoner after their launch landed up the coast near Bayonne.

"Rosa and her men marched us inland, the storm still

lashing us, our limbs weighed down by exhaustion and sorrow at our mates lost and killed. Finally, we reached a farm where we were hurried inside a barn and down a ladder to a root cellar. Only after we were shut in, guards posted, did we risk lighting a few lanterns and got our first good look at each other.

"We were a motley crew, half-drowned and shredded by the storm and ocean. Remember, none of us were true Navy—we'd been merchant sailors pressed to service by the Royal Navy without training, our ship was a supply vessel, no arms at all. Only thing true Navy about us were our officers and there were none among us now, which gave the rabble-rousers a chance to rise up.

"The Irish of us—myself excluded because I had good reason to hate the Krauts after my sis died on the *Athenia*—they favored the Germans, thought if the English lost the war, they'd leave the north and our fight would be won as well. The Scots and Brits, a rough lot gathered from docks across England, most of them no fans of the government and Navy who'd taken our ship and livelihood as their own, were easily swayed by thoughts of leaving the war behind once talk turned of escaping both France and their service."

Cassie closed her eyes, Paddy's words coming to life as if she watched a movie.

PADDY AND HIS men helped themselves to wine their rescuers provided and apples from the baskets lining the dirt walls of the root cellar. There were also bushels of potatoes, turnips, rutabagas, pears, and onions, a harvest safely stored for winter.

"After all, we're none of us real soldiers," Maguire, a socialist from Galway, stood up, leading the debate. No surprise there. Maguire was a loudmouth in all things from berating Cookie for lousy rations to planning the future of Ireland.

The smell of the cellar reminded Paddy of home, of a life led safe on land, no U-boats or curfews or blackouts or weeks of tinned food, the same morning and night, tales of the officers' gourmet fare brought back by the stewards who stole what they could from the upper galley.

Perfect atmosphere for Maguire's talk of mutiny. "Why shouldn't we scamper off, blend in with the civilians, turn our back on this god-forsaken war? The Germans will be winning it soon enough, no reason to put a target on our backs. We didn't ask for this, none of us, right?"

The men sitting at Maguire's feet, crowded into the cramped cellar, nodded and grunted their agreement. Paddy had positioned himself as close to the ladder and escape route as possible, even if it meant missing out on the wine being passed hand-to-hand. He stood, propped against the hard-packed dirt wall, exhausted enough to fall asleep, his head nodding against his chest. On the ship he'd trusted these men, they were his mates, good at their jobs.

But they weren't on board the ship anymore, they were alone, stranded, and without officers to lead them.

Rosa and two of her men stood beside him, near the exit. Protecting them or guarding them? It was clear Rosa spoke English—enough that he could see she followed the debate. It was equally clear that she was disgusted by Maguire's talk of desertion.

As Maguire paced before his rapt and besotted audience, shadows from the lanterns flickering around him, Rosa reached past Padraic to a bushel of turnips, scrounging among them until she found one small enough to fit her hand, almost perfectly round, its body a deep shade of purple, barely a dimple or crease marring it.

Paddy, despite his fatigue, was intrigued enough to shake himself alert. Maguire's speech had reached some impassioned high point that led to cheers from the assembly. He stopped pacing, standing tall as if he'd just been elected Pope, beaming at the men crouched in the dirt before him.

Rosa edged to one side and with a swift movement veiled by the shadows launched the turnip so hard and fast it careened from the side of Maguire's skull with a loud crack.

Maguire, stunned, buckled as his knees gave way. Before his body hit the ground, Rosa was there, an arm around his neck, knife held to his throat.

"Is this your idea of loyalty?" she asked the suddenly silent crowd. "Are you all cowards? Not a man among you ready to fight the bastards who killed your comrades?"

The men stirred, a few having the good grace to look sheepishly at the ground. But there was just Rosa and two of her men between them and an end to their war—at least that's what Maguire had promised them. After being half-drowned, almost dying for a crown they served reluctantly, who was this girl to stand between them and freedom?

A few stood, towering over Rosa. Paddy glanced at her men who stood beside him. Both remained relaxed, one of them chuckling as he handed a jug of wine to the other. Did they not realize how dangerous his shipmates were? Perhaps they didn't understand English?

Paddy stepped forward into the light to stand beside Rosa. She glanced at him, assessing his threat then dismissed him to focus on the others. Maguire moaned and squirmed in her grasp until she tightened her grip, angling her knife against his jugular. He froze, his eyes dilated with fear, gleaming in the lamplight.

"I will not keep you here," Rosa continued. "Even as my men and I risk our own lives to save your comrades before the Vichy swine sell them to the Nazis. I will not threaten, I will not ask you to stay and fight with us. We do not fight alongside cowards and traitors. You are all free to go."

She threw her arms open, releasing Maguire with a shove that sent him sprawling into the laps of the' men before him.

"Now?" an anonymous voice came from the crowd.

"Into the storm?"

"With no food or water?"

"Or map? We've no idea where we are."

"Come on, mates," cried another. "Forget this French bitch. We'll make our own way."

"There's sure to be provisions in the farm house," another said. "Look around. They obviously had a good harvest."

"Not to mention weapons, clothing."

"Women," another suggested, his tone jovial.

"Why wait?" Maguire said, spinning to face Rosa. "Why not start with this wench?"

Rosa stood straighter, her smile an unpleasant sight that sent the hairs on the back of Paddy's neck tingling. He couldn't believe these were the men he'd served side by side with, now talking rape and pillage of the very people who had just saved their lives.

"So, now, you'd be contemplating raping this girl, Jimmy Maguire?" Paddy demanded. "And what would your good wife and your own daughter say to that, do you think? Your gal, she's what, eleven? Wouldn't she be proud of her da? And you, Donald Kraven, wasn't it you who told me how thankful you were that your ole mam was being taken care of by neighbors while you were gone? You'd repay the charity of these who risked their lives to save yours by turning on them?" He strode forward, positioning himself between Rosa and the crowd. "I'm ashamed to know any of you, talk like that."

"You've no love of the English yerself, Paddy Hart," Maguire said. "Why should we risk our lives to save a bunch of officers? We didn't sign on to fight nobody's war."

"Then do as the girl said. Take your leave. But you leave here and now and without a fuss, hear me?" Paddy held his arms out wide, fists bunched, making himself appear bigger. One man against thirty; wouldn't be much of a fight, but it would give Rosa and her men time to get up the ladder and escape.

The ladder behind him creaked as someone climbed it and rapped on the door hidden in the barn's floor. A few minutes later, a gust of night air blew into the cellar. The men cowered, raising their arms high in surrender.

Paddy glanced behind him and saw why. While he'd been chattering on, trying to reach the numbskulls with his gift of gab, Rosa had taken a far more practical approach. She'd sent her men up the ladder and out into the barn while she climbed onto the upended bushel of turnips. In her hand she held one of the kerosene lanterns aloft. Not to light the low-ceilinged cellar draped in shadows. Rather, she gripped the lantern by its base, ready to hurl it into the huddle of suddenly silent men.

"You," she nodded to Paddy. "Padraic Hart. You go. Now."

Paddy backed up until he was against the ladder. "Don't do anything rash. They're just exhausted, scared. Give them a night and they'll be right."

"Go," she repeated, never glancing his way, her gaze

focused on the men.

"No. I'll stay with my mates."

That earned him a glare. He stood, his bulk blocking her own exit. Above him her men called down, asking if she wanted help, but she waved them off. "You come with me. Hostage. You behave, nothing happens to them. They behave, nothing happens to you."

Clever girl had an answer for everything. Up close, the lamplight making her features glow, he finally realized how young she was—and how absolutely fearless. He stepped back, giving her a courtly bow—the product of the nuns' class on deportment—and gestured his surrender.

"*Mais oui, mademoiselle*. I am at your command."

CHAPTER 15

"STAY WITH DENISE, the kids," Drake told Jimmy as he headed to the door. If Kasanov was a federal problem, then he sure as hell was getting the feds and all their resources on board. A personal appeal would be more effective than a phone call. "They're safe. Keep them that way."

Unlike his own family. He had no idea why Kasanov had chosen his family as targets or what he wanted from Drake. But one thing Drake was certain of: Kasanov wouldn't live to see the inside of a courtroom if he touched Hart or Muriel.

He'd spent eleven years of his life working to rebalance the scales of justice, to bring some semblance of sanity to the chaos that threatened to drown the world. His father before him had spent over twenty years doing the same thing, died on the job while chasing down a petty thief who'd stolen thirteen dollars and change.

Kasanov had taken much more than that from Drake. And Drake would sacrifice everything he believed in to see Kasanov rot in hell—even if Drake ended up there alongside him.

The certainty burnt like frozen steel twisted in his gut. Cold, hard, implacable truth.

Denise circled her arms around Jimmy's waist before releasing him with a quick peck on the lips. "We'll be fine," she said. "Meet us back home."

Drake heard the undercurrent in her voice and knew what she meant—she wanted her *entire* family home and safe. That included Hart. And Drake. He wasn't as good at hiding his emotions as he thought if Denise was assigning Jimmy to him as a watchdog.

Jimmy rubbed his cheek along her head, mussing her sleek, blond hair. Then he stood straight and stepped away. "Come on, partner."

"Wait!" Tessa's voice commanded them from the top of the stairs. "I need to talk to you, Drake."

Drake sighed. The old woman was a dear friend but he had no time for her rambling stories and homilies. Not while a madman held his mother and Hart. "I'll be back," he assured her.

She frowned as if listening to an unheard inner voice. "All right then. But don't wait too long." They started through the door and she called out. "And bring Cassandra with you!"

Drake paused, his shoulders hunching against Tessa's tone of certainty. It was too painful to hope he'd get either Muriel or Hart back at all, much less in a condition to go on social calls. Almost easier to imagine them already dead—to start accepting, preparing against the harsh reality.

He was a cop, had seen it all. There was no way they were alive, he told himself as he stumbled out the door. Each word struck like a bullet, bouncing off the newly forged steel in his belly. He repeated them, tempering, hardening himself. Each word was also a promise—a vow that Kasanov would pay dearly.

"Don't give up on Hart, kid." Andy's voice startled him. The ex-cop stood up from where he waited on Tessa's porch swing. "She'd tell you never to give up—Lord knows she never gave up on you."

Drake stared at his friend, his father's old partner, the man who had first trained him to be a cop. Where had this sudden optimism come from? What happened to the cop whose first words of advice to his rookie partner had been, "You can't take everything to heart. Learn to let it bounce off like you're wearing Kevlar on the inside. You take it home and you won't be long for this job or this world, kid."

Pretty much the way Drake's father had handled the trauma of the job. Probably why he died of a heart attack at such a young age.

Words failing, Drake shook his head at Andy and continued on to his car. He didn't have time for philosophy right now, couldn't spare the energy for hope.

Then a woman's voice came to him. *Life is hope, love is faith.*

He almost dropped the keys as he whirled. Hart's voice, whispering something her gypsy grandmother had once told her. He looked around, ready to cry for real this time. Christ, she'd sounded so close, so real—was he losing it?

Or was she already dead? Haunting him? Hart believed in things like that, thought Rosa's ghost lived with her.

"You want me to drive?" Jimmy asked from the opposite side of the car. Drake merely shook his head, still stunned. She was dead. No, she couldn't be dead, not Hart. She was dead. No. Never. The debate roared in his mind.

Hope for the best, prepare for the worst. That was Muriel—how many times had he heard that from her? Before every algebra test that he'd spend all night cramming for, every time the phone rang in the middle of the night when his dad was on the streets, that awful sun-filled spring day when the doorbell had rung for real, giving her the news of Drake Senior's death.

That's when he realized they were together. Which meant Hart would protect Muriel, with her life if need be. Together, they had a chance of making it out of this alive.

Drake opened the car door just as a uniformed officer he didn't recognize came running up. "I've got a witness," he panted, pointing down the street to the house on the corner. "Two black Town Cars. The older woman was taken in one that headed east and the lady in the wedding dress was in the second. They headed north."

Jimmy moved to intercept the officer as Drake slumped against the car. So much for hope.

He fell into the driver's seat. The Mustang rocked as Jimmy added his weight to the passenger side. He felt Jimmy's gaze on him but kept his own eyes locked forward, not acknowledging his partner's look of concern. Jimmy said nothing; what was there to say? They both knew the statistics, both knew how these things usually ended.

Drake prayed they were alive, but in the meantime, he was insulating his heart in Kevlar. Getting ready to sell his soul to the devil. Because what did being a cop, what did anything matter if Kasanov killed the women he loved?

AFTER WHAT SEEMED like hours, the car came to a stop. But no one moved to release Cassie. She heard muffled sounds beyond her prison inside the trunk but could make out no words. Then there was silence and she feared they'd left her to die.

She fought to hold the panic at bay, retreating to her favorite childhood memories, and when those didn't work, she relived, minute by minute, second by second, every moment she could remember with Drake.

Finally, the trunk lid flew open and a blinding light

stabbed her eyes. Rough hands reached inside and hauled her out.

Her legs were frozen, asleep from their cramped position. Two men, neither older than twenty, placed her on her feet then removed their hands, laughing as she tumbled onto a concrete floor, unable to catch herself with her hands bound behind her back. She ignored their laughter, blinking hard, trying to focus her mind and her body.

Cassie took inventory. Her mouth was parched, her bladder full, left arm numb from the elbow down, right hand with a painful tingling in it, both legs spasming beneath her.

Equipment and hydraulic lifts surrounded her. She was lying on a grease-stained floor of an industrial garage. What time was it? How long had she been trapped in the car?

She jerked her head up. Where was Muriel?

"Muriel," the name scraped out her throat, her voice rough as gravel.

"Mrs. Drake will not be joining us at this time."

Cassie twisted her body to face the direction the voice had come from. Twenty feet away, Kasanov sat on a leather club chair, his tailored suit draping his body in silk, a cigar in one hand and a sapphire-colored bottle of water in the other. Cassie's eyes riveted on the water, following it as he nonchalantly set it on the small table beside him.

They were inside a large service bay designed for several vehicles, including pits beneath hydraulic hoists;

chains dangling from pulleys overhead, ending in heavy, metal hooks; and racks of tools. The only vehicle was the Ford she'd arrived in. There were four garage doors, all closed, one exit door at the far end of the bay, and a door behind Kasanov's chair that appeared to lead to an office and customer reception area from what she could see through the window beside the door.

"I would expect you're quite thirsty by this time, Dr. Hart. Would you like some water? I have it imported from Switzerland. It's quite refreshing." He dangled a second bottle like a dog biscuit.

Cassie pushed herself up into kneeling position. Her left arm was now pins and needles, shooting darts of pain, but her legs were still useless, quivering masses of over-strained muscles. She bit her lip against the painful cramping in her thighs and tried to find enough saliva to swallow.

"Where's Muriel?" She managed to not clamp down on the words as a spasm shot through her right leg.

"I assure you she's perfectly safe. If you're not thirsty, I'll just pour the water out."

If she'd been able to make any tears, Cassie would have cried as he twisted the cap off one of the bottles and tilted it. The life-giving essence dripped out slowly at first then in a stream, forming an oil-slicked puddle on the cement floor. The bottle empty, Kasanov let it drop to the floor, breaking it into thousands of shards of blue glass glistening in the harsh fluorescent lights.

"I ask you once again, Dr. Hart." He uncapped the second precious bottle. "Would you like some water?"

Don't be a fool. Rosa's voice broke through her resolve. *You need to keep your strength up. Get the water, fight later.*

"Yes," Cassie cried as the first precious drops spilled from the bottle.

Kasanov smiled and righted the bottle. "Very well. Come and have a drink."

Should have seen that one coming, Cassie chided herself. It was impossible, but to salvage some of her pride, she attempted to climb to her feet. She used the bumper of the car for leverage, pressing her bound hands against it. She made it almost to a standing position before her legs gave out, dumping her back onto the floor. Kasanov's men chuckled from their positions behind her.

Keeping her eyes focused on the sapphire bottle of hope, Cassie dragged her body across the grease-stained floor.

CHAPTER 16

Jimmy didn't complain as Drake drove over the curb and down the sidewalk before bouncing around a patrol car and back onto the street. He dug the red light out of the glove box and set it, revolving, on the dashboard. They made the drive to the FBI's offices across the river in record time.

Drake never said a word the entire trip, which gave Jimmy the time to pave their way with a few phone calls. He'd figured on browbeating some junior agent stuck with duty on the Friday before Christmas, but mention Kasanov's name and next thing he knew, it was the head of the Organized Crime task force, a supervisory special agent named Prescott, on the line.

By the time they arrived, security badges and a fresh-scrubbed junior G-man named Taylor were waiting in the lobby, ready to escort Drake and Jimmy upstairs to the inner sanctum.

"What I don't understand," a middle-aged man with salt and pepper hair was saying as they were led into a high-tech situation room, "is why Kasanov didn't just kill them all?" He looked up when Drake and Jimmy appeared but didn't soften his tone. You want in, you'd better be wearing body armor, his expression said.

This must be Prescott. Guy dressed like a movie mafia don and looked like he was leading a hostile takeover of a rival corporation rather than a hastily convened emergency briefing.

"Why leave any witnesses?" Prescott continued. The other two agents in the room with him, neither of who looked old enough to vote, both nodded eagerly.

"He wants something," Jimmy said, ignoring the federal agents and helping himself to a cup of their coffee. Drake moved to a corner where he could see all the players and have a good view of the computer screen projected onto the far wall. This placed him behind Prescott, but the fed didn't seem bothered by having a non-feebie at his back.

"Obvious," came the clipped tones of a peaches-and-cream female agent, her accent hailing from Texas or Oklahoma. She looked like she should be leading a pep rally instead of discussing a violent crime lord. "But what?"

Prescott answered. "Depends on who was the target.

Cassandra Hart or Detective Drake."

"Hart's a doctor at a community clinic. What could she have of value to Kasanov?"

"Maybe something he thinks Hart has seen or knows, but," Jimmy took a sip of coffee and thought for a moment, "he's not entirely certain. And that's why he didn't kill anyone at the party. Maybe he was worried he'd be killing the one person who could force Hart to do whatever it is he wants."

"Then he'd have done better to take one of the juveniles as his second hostage," the other agent, one who obviously wasn't aware Jimmy was father of two of those "juveniles," put in in a bland tone. He had Hispanic coloring and a shaven head that made Jimmy look twice for gang tattoos, even though he knew visible body art was against FBI policy.

Prescott cleared his throat as Jimmy crushed the paper cup and hurled it at a garbage can just past the agent's head. The junior agent jerked up at that, shooting Jimmy a narrow-eyed glare.

"Maybe I should introduce our guests before we continue," Prescott said. "This is Detective Jimmy Dolan of Pittsburgh's Major Case Squad." Shaven-head lowered his gaze and pretended to be engrossed in his notes. "Father of two of our witnesses and husband to Denise Dolan, also a witness. And, for those of you who haven't recognized him, Detective Mickey Drake."

"It was my mother and fiancée Kasanov took," Drake

put in, his voice as expressionless as his face. In Jimmy's experience, that blank void of a stare always meant trouble. Kid shut down like that, meant the powder keg's fuse was lit and burning fast.

"Makes more sense if Drake is the real target," Texas said in a chipper voice as if this tidbit of enlightenment would solve all their problems. "His paintings burned, his family taken. Maybe Kasanov is tied to a former case? From the Interpol report, Kasanov has been known to carry a grudge against prosecutors and judges who target him."

"Do you people have anything?" Drake asked, turning to the small task force. "Besides vague theories?"

"The only thing we know for certain about Kasanov is to expect the unexpected," Taylor, the agent who'd acted as their escort, put in. Despite his youth, he must have some seniority because Prescott shifted the computer over to him.

Kasanov's photo, one that appeared several years old, flashed onto the monitor. "Nickolai Bernard Kasanov—at least that's his current incarnation," he began. "Real name unknown. There's a list of his aliases in your briefing packets. Date of birth, unknown, suspected to be approximately 1940 or 1941. Place of birth unknown, but phonetic analysis of vocal patterns place his origins in the Austria-Hungarian area. Parents—"

"Unknown," Jimmy interrupted, saving Drake the effort. "Cut the crap. What *do* you know?"

Taylor's eyes sparked but he continued without pause. "Known to have been involved in fifty-three homicides.

Suspected in another thirty-one."

"Jeezit—what's this actor doing out on the streets?" Jimmy asked with indignation. "Seventy-four people he's killed and you're letting him get away with it?"

"Those all occurred outside of the USA," Texas said.

Prescott placed both his hands flat on the table, drawing the attention of all of the agents. "That's one of the things that worries me. While he has criminal enterprises running here, Kasanov has never stepped foot on US soil before. And we can't find any trace that he has now. If he's here, he's a ghost."

"Are we sure it's him?" Shaven-head said, risking a glance in Jimmy's direction.

In answer, Jimmy tossed Jacob's phone to him. "See for yourself." As the junior agents gathered around the video, Jimmy turned to Prescott. "Seems like Kasanov knows how to stay off the radar. Any ideas why he's coming out in the open now?"

"He's fighting a war," Taylor, the computer guy, said. "And losing."

"These Eastern European mobs are always fighting over something," Jimmy scoffed. "Remember the bootleg vodka war two years ago?"

"This one is more serious," Prescott answered. "Kasanov is strictly old-school. Strong-arm tactics, kidnapping, blackmail, murder for hire. Forget the twenty-first century, his business model dates back to Attila the Hun."

Taylor took over, flashing several screens of financial data onto the monitor. "Kasanov has always been fiercely independent. His organization is small, family-based, but used to being feared and respected and brought in plenty of money. Until now."

He leaned back, folding his arms behind his head as if proud of himself. "Welcome to the age of the Internet. Blackmail occurs online. You want to kidnap someone? You hold their hard drive hostage. No need to kill when you can hijack a person's—hell, a company's—bank accounts and siphon off all their money with a click of a button."

"So Kasanov isn't doing well. What's that got to do with Drake?" Jimmy asked. "And why is he here in Pittsburgh?"

No one had an answer to that.

"Tell me about the homicides," Drake said in a low voice, staring at Kasanov's photo as if he and the murderer were the only two people in the room.

"First we can verify was a storekeeper in Prague, 1954. During an attempted armed robbery. He actually did time for that but escaped from custody. Then he moved onto hiring himself out as a leg breaker, worked for various Mafia factions: Sicilians, Corsicans, Greeks, Turks, even Basques at one point. Always staying in Europe and Central Asia, dropping bodies wherever he went."

Drake shook his head. "No, those are all just business. You said he was unpredictable. Tell me about the murders that don't fit the pattern."

Jimmy moved to join his partner, nodding in approval. Two great minds think alike. Even when one was clouded with worry.

No, more than worry; worry was what Jimmy felt. Stark terror was more like what Drake was experiencing, Jimmy thought as he saw the muscles at the corner of Drake's jaw spasm. He swore he could hear Drake's teeth grind in frustration as they waited for the FBI's best and brightest to give them the answers they needed. That break in Drake's facade made Jimmy worry even more.

Taylor fiddled with his computer for moment, then a screen with a dozen thumbnail photos appeared. He clicked on each on in turn, blowing it up to the full view.

"These all seem unmotivated," he told them. "The first documented was a prostitute in Budapest. Found dead after spending a night with a man identified as Kasanov." A mug shot photo appeared, the woman was in her mid-thirties, old for a prostitute—especially to attract a man like Kasanov, Jimmy thought.

"He was what, twenty, then?"

"Try seventeen," Texas answered. "I'm sure the BAU would label these homicides as the pleasure kills of a sadist who enjoys ritual torture."

Taylor flashed another image. Another tortured woman. And another. Until finally, he projected a map of the killings. A bloody trail leading across Europe, the former Soviet Union, and Central Asia.

The footsteps of a psychopathic serial killer who hated

women. Jimmy took a drink of his coffee, mainly to cover his emotions, but it turned to acid in his mouth. This was the man who had Drake's mother and Hart.

And they had no idea why he'd targeted them or what he wanted.

Chapter 17

ONCE CASSIE REACHED his feet, Kasanov jerked his head in a nod and one of his minions leapt forward, knife in hand, and cut her wrists free. She stretched for the bottle of water Kasanov held out to her. Finally, she grasped it with both hands, fearful that she might drop it, her fingers were so numb.

Greedily, she drank it all before he could change his mind. She would have tried to maintain her dignity, but she couldn't survive without water. Besides, what did she care about humiliation? Didn't matter one wit what Kasanov and his men thought of her as long as it got her what she wanted: her and Muriel safe and free.

Was this how Rosa felt when the Gestapo held her prisoner? Paddy had dropped hints of that time, but Cassie never heard Rosa say a word about it, had to fill in any details from her imagination colored by horrors described in the history books.

But, just like Paddy had come for Rosa, she knew Drake would rally every law enforcement agency and use all their resources to find her and Muriel.

She scanned her environment. The window behind Kasanov, the one leading to the office area, was now crowded with faces pressed against the glass. Children of all ages—the pickpockets she'd seen last night at the museum. She didn't see the woman, Natasha, or the boy, Vincent, but then the door from the office slid open silently, just far enough to allow a reedy-thin boy to slip through. Vincent. He sidled into the shadows behind Kasanov and his men to stand, waiting, watching.

Good to know she had one ally here. The thought brought with it strength.

As she tilted the bottle back to suck out the final drops, she glanced at Kasanov. He lounged in his chair, watching her with an indulgent smile, not hurried at all.

Didn't he know he'd already lost? There was no way he could escape. What good was any story of Rosa's past when he'd be spending the rest of his life in prison? If Drake didn't kill him first.

The thought made her want to smile, but she forced it back. Kasanov couldn't have come as far as he had without being smart enough to have an exit strategy. Which meant her job would be to stall him as long as possible, give Drake the time he needed to find her and Muriel.

She glanced at the men with guns. Only four of them, none old enough to drink legally; one of them didn't even look like he'd started shaving yet. Why so young? Wouldn't a man like Kasanov have more experienced thugs at his command? Maybe the younger men were more pliable, willing to do violence for no good reason?

Or maybe they were expendable? Probably both. She wondered if there was some way she could use that against them.

She set the bottle down. Kasanov said nothing. Okay, she'd play his game, act the supplicant. "Thank you," she said, her voice raspy.

He inclined his head as if granting a royal boon. And waited.

"May I see Muriel?" she asked. "I'd like to make sure she's okay."

"You doubt my word?" he boomed, but his frown was fake. All part of the damn game.

"No. Of course not." Right. Like she trusted the word of a man who'd threatened to kill a child in front of his mother. "May I please see her?"

"I think not. Not until I've received some cooperation for my efforts."

"I don't understand." Cassie shifted her weight as her legs began to come alive with pain. Her ankles were still bound so she had no choice but to sit like a child, legs curled up to one side or the other.

"Rosa never told you about the treasure she stole?"

"No. She never talked about her past."

He made a skeptical noise. "What about that *gaje* she married? Padraic Hart. What did he tell you?"

"He used to tell me stories about the people they helped escape from the Nazis, about some of the things they did during the war. Nothing about any treasure."

He said nothing, glaring at her with mistrust. She took a chance, tried to keep him talking. "You're Lowara, right? Weren't your people there when Rosa's kumpania was attacked in 1936?" According to Paddy, the Lowara betrayed Rosa's family to the Germans, but she held that back. "Is that when the treasure was lost? Because Rosa barely escaped with her life—she had nothing when the Germans took her."

"Not then. Later. During the war. She and Padraic Hart stole something so immense, so valuable that they killed my grandfather to protect their secret. It's taken me all this time to piece together the clues that led me to you— all I had was Rosa's name and the fact she murdered my father in Paris on Christmas Eve, 1940."

Cassie remained silent, unsure what to say that wouldn't provoke him. He was a muscular man, trim, in good shape, but when he spoke of Rosa, his color flushed and the veins in his neck swelled. High blood pressure, she diagnosed. Would it be too much to ask for a stroke sometime soon? Didn't have to kill him, just incapacitate him long enough for her to escape.

No one answered her prayer and he continued. "You may think Rosa Costello was a hero, but she was nothing more than a thief and an assassin, betraying one of her own for the sake of her *gaje* lover." He spat, the wad of mucus hitting Cassie's chest, sliding along the bodice of Muriel's once-beautiful dress. To mix with *gaje*, outsiders, was the worst sin a Rom woman could commit, leaving her forever *marhime*, unclean, shunned.

Cassie thought hard. She had to stall, but she did not have the answers Kasanov sought. "I think Rosa killed many men during the war," she said softly. "I'm not sure which was your father. But I will tell you what I know."

"Tell me all of it. The truth. Any lies or deception and Mrs. Drake suffers."

She nodded her agreement. Playing Scheherazade with a psychopath, Muriel's life in the balance—and her only weapons the tall tales her grandfather had spun when she was a child.

Drake had better find them. Fast.

CHAPTER 18

IN A SURREAL turn, Rosa escorted Paddy through the barn while her men stayed behind to guard his shipmates. At first he'd balked. "I'll not be given any special treatment. I'll stay with my mates."

But then she turned that witchy smile of hers on him and asked, "The ones who wanted to rape me and pillage this farm?"

"They're scared is all. They've just had their ship shot out from under them, ended up practically behind enemy lines." After all, unoccupied France was more an idea than an absolute.

Her eyes flared in judgment over his fellow sailors but she said nothing. Instead, she took his arm and led him outside into the night. The storm had moved east, lightning blazing through the sky in the distance, but immediately overhead the sky was clearing, only a few ragged clouds obscuring the moon.

His clothing still sodden and heavy, exhaustion dimming his awareness, he walked with her across a yard, looking back over his shoulder to the barn where his men were now captives.

Rosa touched his arm. "They'll be safe. You have my word."

What choice did he have? They reached the house where Rosa knocked gently on the kitchen door. It opened almost immediately, revealing a buxom, middle-aged woman and her stoutly built husband. If not for the rapid-fire French they spewed as they each took turns clutching Rosa with hearty embraces, they would have been at home in any Connemara cottage. Paddy shuffled his feet, uncertain what to do or say, then was surprised when as soon as the couple finished greeting Rosa, they pulled him inside and embraced him just as warmly.

"*Merci*," he stuttered. "*Merci beaucoup.*"

More French followed, and after a few minutes, he got the hang of their rhyme and accent, so very different from the schoolboy French the officers had taught him or the clipped radio reports he'd intercepted. Rosa beamed as he answered them, haltingly at first, then more relaxed, recounting the events of the night. The husband, Jean-Marie, sat Paddy down at a seat beside the kitchen fire, while his wife doled out hearty vegetable stew.

When he'd eaten his fill—feeling a bit guilty, but the lads had done it to themselves, acting the way they had—he sat back, finally warm for the first time that night. Rosa stared at him with an appraising glance, and then threw him a question. "How was the food?"

He answered automatically before realizing she'd spoken in German. So had he. The farmers exchanged glances, but Rosa smiled and nodded. She stood and embraced the man and woman, telling them good night. The couple shuffled off to bed.

Once it was just he and Rosa, she jerked her chin, indicating he should stand. She walked around him as if measuring him for a funeral suit. As she stood behind him, Paddy remembered how quick she'd been with the knife when she'd tackled Maguire. But surely she wouldn't waste good food on a man she intended to kill.

"How did you learn French and German?" she asked, returning to her seat across the table from him. She did hold her knife in her hand, playing with it, spinning it across her fingers and around again in a flash.

"I worked in the radio shack. Whenever we overheard transmissions from the Germans or French—before you all scuttled your own navy, that is—"

"I'm not French," she interrupted him. "But go on."

"Anyway, I'd repeat the messages for the watch officer. They realized I could repeat anything I heard, so thought it best if I could understand them myself in case there was an intercept that required immediate action. So the officers took me on as a pet project, teaching me French and German."

She nodded. Sat in silent thought for another few minutes. "Do you know anything about the Nazis—their rank structure, what their uniform insignias mean?"

He shrugged. "There are posters in the radio shack and the mess. Know the enemy. Mainly Jane's, ships and U-boats, airplane silhouettes, the like." He leaned forward, elbows on the table, his face mere inches from hers. "If you're planning a rescue mission, want to save the rest of my crew, I'm game."

A slow smile spread across her features—even in this short time he'd already discovered that when she smiled, it was with her entire body, not just her lips. He decided he liked making her smile, vowed to do it as often as possible.

"I believe you are." She pushed her chair back. "Right then. Let's get a move on."

Rosa led Paddy back to the barn where her men were circled around a lantern, keeping watch over the door to the root cellar. Paddy felt a flush of shame at the way his crew had acted earlier. He tried to blame it on the events of the night combined with exhaustion and the wine, not to mention the adrenalin that came with finding yourself stranded in a foreign country, your fate suddenly in your own hands.

Still, he wondered how much faith he could place in the men he'd served with. The thought brought with it a mixture of guilt at doubting but also an awareness of the life-and-death stakes he faced. Not just him—Rosa and her people as well. One blathering idiot or hothead looking to get back at Rosa for humiliating him in front of the rest of the crew could doom them all.

God, he was bone-weary. And from Rosa's hints, the night had just begun. The weight of responsibility settled over his shoulders. Every decision he made from here on out would impact so many lives. He wasn't an officer, wasn't suited for command. He just wanted to do his job, help fight the Krauts, pay them back for killing his sis, and keep himself and his crew alive. Was that too much to ask?

"Any problems?" Rosa asked.

"No," one of the Frenchmen answered. "They're asleep."

"Good. Make sure you get something to eat and some rest." She turned to the man she shared the guttural language with. Said something and he left, returning with a bundle of clothing he thrust at Paddy. He seemed skeptical, talking rapidly and gesturing with his hands as if measuring Paddy's shoulders. Rosa translated. "Fernando thinks you're too skinny to impersonate a German officer."

Impersonate a German? That'd buy you the firing squad for sure. Paddy unfolded the top layer of clothing and found an officer's uniform and wool overcoat. Not just any officer. Even he recognized the insignia of the SS.

Rosa and the man kept talking then she turned to him. "I told him you'd make a fine officer. Show him a salute."

Fernando glowered at Paddy and he realized the man

didn't care one wit about Paddy's fate—he was worried Paddy would botch the job and get Rosa killed. Paddy straightened and gave his best impression of an officer, snapping at Fernando in German. "Officers do not salute. We are saluted. Show some respect."

The other man raised an eyebrow, shrugged one shoulder then turned to Rosa with the universal hand gesture of maybe, maybe not. Rosa smiled and turned to the other man. "We need to get going. Is Dex ready?"

"He's waiting for you behind the barn. What should we do with this lot?" He nodded to the cellar door.

"Come daybreak show them the route at Banyuls. Then you return to Marseilles. We'll meet you there tomorrow night."

"Do you trust them?"

She shrugged. "It's a well-marked trail, they won't need a guide."

Paddy intervened. "Wait. Where are you taking my men?"

"Not taking. Sending. Over the mountains into Spain. From there, they can give themselves up and the Spanish will turn them over to your consulate. It's the safest way to protect them from the Germans without risking my people."

"If the Spanish are so eager to help, why can't all our soldiers escape that way?" Paddy had overheard the ship's officers talking about the dangers RAF pilots faced when shot down over France, even unoccupied France.

"Your men aren't combatants," she reminded him.

"Merchant sailors, they don't carry military identification. The Spanish will most likely treat them the same as they do the civilian refugees we shepherd across the border. Worst thing they could do is put them in prison, but even then, once your consulate found out, they'd make diplomatic arrangements."

Paddy wasn't convinced. "You've done this before. With merchant sailors like us?"

"No. But it's the safest thing for everyone." She seemed to somehow grow in height as she met his gaze. "If you disagree, you are all welcome to wait here. We'll keep you fed as best we can, for as long as we can."

"Prisoners. You want to keep us prisoners?"

"Until my people are safely away and there's no one your men can betray." She crossed her arms over her chest and stood silent, waiting for his decision.

Shite. Thirty lives waiting for him to see into the future and decide their fate. "Spain," he finally said. She was right—that route created less risk for the civilians here, Rosa's people, as well as his crew. "Send them into Spain."

She nodded, turned on her heel, and crossed the barn to exit out a rear door designed for large equipment and wagons. Paddy stared after her, then looked to her man who was clearly amused at his confusion. "She didn't say anything—"

"Didn't have to. But you'd best hurry if you want to save your officers. Rosa's not one to wait for any man."

CHAPTER 19

⸺ ·≡◈◖◗◈≡· ⸺

DRAKE HAD NOTHING to do.

Activity swirled around him as Prescott called in the rest of his troops. Texas was waking up Interpol contacts halfway around the world, getting more details on Kasanov's past crimes and known associates. The smart-mouthed kid, Taylor, turned out to be some kind of cyber-wiz and was coordinating the local search while simultaneously scanning CC camera footage along Kasanov's escape route. Jimmy was arranging interviews with Alicia Fairstone as well as the people who'd been seated at Kasanov's table at the gala last night.

Drake couldn't stop staring at the photos of the murdered women who'd been found in Kasanov's wake. Nickolai Kasanov, born 1940 or 1941—same time Hart's grandparents had been in France, working against the Nazis. Meant nothing. After all, how many millions of boys were born during those two years?

Still. Rosa. He'd never met her—she'd died four years ago, long before he met Hart. But he'd seen photos of her and Padraic. Hart looked so much like her grandmother it was uncanny.

He jerked upright. All those dead women. They *all* looked like Rosa.

No. He blinked, looked again at the grainy photos, scoured from ancient police and autopsy records. No, they didn't really look like Rosa, did they? Same dark hair, same high cheekbones, but that was commonplace in the locales where Kasanov had hunted.

God, he was losing it. He slumped against a corner of the room, watching Prescott fire orders into two phones he juggled. Was it only two nights ago that he'd been happy? Two nights ago he'd had the promise of *Steadfast*'s debut, the promise of money to build upon the dream come true that was the Liberty Center, the promise of Hart, marrying her, having her for the rest of his life.

The bang of a phone being slammed down shot through the room. Drake jerked upright, hand falling to his gun.

"Son of a bitch," Taylor said.

A spike of terror impaled itself in Drake's heart. Dead. They were both dead.

He turned to the window, hiding his face, blinking

back emotion, pretending to be absorbed in the twilight-cloaked skyline visible across the river.

God, what was he going to do? He wanted to howl, scream, to pummel and destroy—to inflict the pain he felt on someone else.

Instead, he turned, spine held ramrod straight, shoulders hunched against the expected blow. "What?"

Taylor finished his notation in the log and looked around, surprised every eye in the room was on him. "I found where they made the first car switch." His fingers tapped and a map appeared on the screen, tracing Kasanov's route. A red arrow blinked.

"Three Rivers Medical Center," Jimmy said. "The arrogant sonofa—"

Drake closed his eyes for a split second, trying to reorient his soul. There was still a chance, they may still be alive, a whisper of hope blew through his mind.

One way or the other he had to know—he didn't think he could survive much more of this.

"Do we have visual confirmation?" Prescott barked at his junior G-man.

"Yes, sir, downloading from the security office at Three Rivers now. Their cameras are on a three-second scan, so it'll look little choppy." He shut up as the images filled the screen.

Drake felt his heart lurch as he saw his mother being manhandled from the back of a Town Car and then placed into the rear seat of a Toyota Avalon. She looked fine, other than the look of terror etched into her face. They drove off and vanished from sight.

A few frames later Kasanov jerked Hart from an identical Town Car. Even in the grainy black-and-white images, Drake could see blood splattering her face and dress, more than what he'd seen in the earlier images of her at Tessa's. His fists tightened and he took an involuntary step forward as if he could vent his rage on Kasanov in person instead of observing impassively from a distance.

The image flicked again, the men leading Hart to a pale gray minivan.

"That a girl," Jimmy whispered in the silent room. Prescott nodded in agreement—somehow in the few seconds it had taken her to cross the pavement, Hart had spotted the security camera and made a point to stare at it, her back momentarily to her abductors. In the next frame, she was being shoved into the rear of the Dodge Caravan— her hand planted firmly on the roof of the gray vehicle.

The same blood-smeared hand she'd held out to the camera in the previous frame.

"What was the time on that?" Prescott asked, his eyes cutting to the window and the rapidly setting sun. He didn't wait for Taylor's answer but grabbed his phone. "Tell the copters to stay out, sweep a pattern from Three Rivers Medical Center. Gray Caravan, don't bother with the plates, they'll change them, but there's a bloody handprint on the roof. I know they won't be able to see that in the dark, so tell them to hustle before it is dark!"

"Sir, this footage is almost two hours old," Taylor said, his voice contrite.

"Goddamn it! Why didn't those rent-a-cops at Three Rivers pick this up earlier?" Prescott flared.

"Kasanov was there during change of shift," Taylor explained. "And the parking level they used was supposed to be closed. It's scheduled to be repainted, so it wasn't on the live feed monitors."

"Who knew about the painting? Let's get someone working on that," Texas suggested. Drake still hadn't caught her name—and really didn't care.

The older law enforcement officers in the room merely shook their heads. "It'll be a dead end," Jimmy told her. "We need something to give us an idea where Kasanov is heading next, not how he knew where to go hours ago."

"Oh." She looked crestfallen as she returned to her own assignment.

Drake glanced out the window, the sun setting a new speed record as it slid to the horizon. Think you could cut us a break here? he sped the prayer out to the heavens, not really caring who or what was there to hear it, as long as it was answered.

✺

AS CASSIE SPUN her tale of that first wild night when Rosa rescued Padraic and then together they plotted to rescue the rest of his crew, she realized there was one good thing about being held captive by a madman while wearing your wedding dress. The billowing skirts hid her legs along with the shards of glass she slid beneath them every time she shifted position.

That glass bottle Kasanov had broken in order to torment her was going to win her a chance to escape.

CHAPTER 20

Paddy followed Rosa out to the back of the barn where he was surprised to find an ambulance parked under the trees. A skinny man in his early twenties lounged in the driver's seat but leapt out and snapped to attention when he saw Paddy. "*Heil* Hitler!" He saluted as he gave Rosa a wink.

Rosa ignored him and went behind the ambulance. A few minutes later she returned, her trousers and sweater exchanged for a German nurse's uniform. "Get changed, Major Strauss," she ordered Paddy. "We need to get a move on."

"What's all this about?" Paddy asked the driver as he changed in the rear of the fully equipped ambulance. Two stretchers were in place along either wall with room for two more to hang above them. Rosa stayed outside, giving her men last-minute instructions while the driver scrutinized a map in the front seat.

"You didn't think we came all the way here on the off chance that some Brits would need rescuing, did you?" the driver answered. "We're on a mission. Rescuing some downed RAF pilots from the hospital at Villa Chagrin." His accent was American and he turned to Paddy with a grin. "They call me Dex—don't ask me why. Real name is Linus."

"Padraic—Paddy." The uniform was a decent fit but Paddy stopped when he saw a spot of blood on the back of the shirt collar.

"Rosa's got the technique down pat," Dex said. "Dagger to the base of the skull. Silent, fast, and hardly any blood unless you remove it too soon." He turned the whole way around, facing Paddy, gauging his reaction. "Which she had to do when the other one surprised us." He opened his uniform jacket revealing a pink stain over the chest of his uniform shirt. "Haven't been able to get it all the way out."

Paddy considered that. That slight girl with blood on her hands—not just anyone's blood, a German officer. "How many men has she killed?" It was an insane question and he wasn't sure he wanted the answer.

Dex shrugged. "Not sure. She's been in this war longer than any of us. Started back in '36 when the Germans killed her family and sent her to a prison camp."

"Her entire family? Why?"

"She's Roma—gypsy. Before the Germans targeted the

Jews, they tried to exterminate the gypsies. They built camps, using them as slave labor. Those who fought back, like Rosa's family, they massacred. Guess it was practice for what they're doing now with the Jews. You know the Germans, so damn efficient."

Paddy had heard the officers talk about rumors of death camps and forced marches as the Germans rounded up the Jews within their borders, but he—and the officers— had dismissed it as propaganda. He glanced out the rear door in the direction Rosa had gone. To see your entire family butchered simply for who they were. It was as insane as the Troubles in the north—his mother's family was from Ulster and caught up in the fighting there.

"You're American. Why are you doing this?" Paddy gestured to the bloodstained uniforms they both wore.

Dex leaned back, his gaze distant. "Charlie and I started in Paris. We were taking a year off after Yale, pretending to take classes at the Sorbonne, but really just kicking loose before we started working for our fathers. Mine's on Wall Street—you've no earthly idea how much I dread being manacled by stocks and bonds and paperwork. Anyway, we were caught there when the Germans invaded, decided to do some good, so joined the American Volunteer Ambulance Corps. One thing led to another and we found ourselves transporting refugees, made it south to the border—more luck than anything, well, also the French are the most unorganized people on the face of the planet—and thankfully stumbled into one of Rosa's operations before we got everyone killed."

"So you decided to impersonate German officers and use your ambulance to rescue British prisoners?"

"Decide is a strong word. Rosa had an idea and she is extremely hard to say no to. Truth be told, Charlie and I both jumped at the chance. It was an adventure. We'd kicked around Germany, so both spoke the language. All we needed was to repaint the ambulance and grab a few uniforms, legit papers."

Paddy finished dressing in the dead man's uniform just as Rosa climbed into the rear of the ambulance and shut the doors. Dex started driving.

"Fits him better than the Basque," Dex said as he drove the vehicle across the farm lane's rutted, frozen mud. Paddy quickly realized they hadn't chosen him simply because he spoke German. The dead man had been tall like Paddy with broader than average shoulders. All those years working the boat and nets with his da had left Paddy's chest and shoulders built up so they fit the major's uniform perfectly.

"The Basque?" Paddy asked, hanging onto the strap bolted to the wall as the vehicle lurched from the dirt lane onto a paved road.

"Fernando," Rosa said. Ah, that explained the strange language. How many languages did Rosa speak? She eyed Paddy appraisingly. "He's no Charlie."

Dex sighed and glanced at Rosa in the mirror. "No one is." They both were silent for a moment, mourning a fallen comrade—Paddy knew the look, the tone. So it wasn't just one man who'd died wearing this uniform. What was he getting into?

Rosa reached behind her and handed Paddy a bundle of papers. "Memorize everything in here."

He glanced at them: official identification, transit pass, and several letters, some handwritten, some typed on Nazi letterheads. He was now Major Heinrich Strauss. Inside one of the handwritten letters was a photo of a tall blond woman and two small girls clinging to her skirts.

Fear lit his gut on fire. Despite Dex's cavalier attitude, this wasn't simple playacting on a lark.

"I can't read German," he finally admitted. He shoved the papers back at Rosa. "Read them aloud to me and I'll remember." No one needed to mention that their lives depended on his memory and acting skills.

Rosa didn't accept the papers. Instead she turned away, shoulders drooping. Dex pulled the ambulance to a stop. "No worries," he said. "Rosa, you drive. I'll coach our Irishman. After all, I did play the lead in *Hamlet* back at New Haven."

Situation diffused, they traded places and resumed their journey. Paddy was reminded once again how young Rosa was. It was clear that although she spoke several languages, like him, it was a verbal skill. Could she read and write at all? If she was really was gypsy, like the travelers back home, then maybe not. How could a girl with no formal education have any chance going up against the well-trained Nazis?

Dex diverted his thoughts as they began to chat in German. "Tell me about yourself," he started. "What's your favorite hobby, Major Strauss?"

Padraic froze. Hobbies? He had no hobbies.

Dex read his anxiety. "Relax, man. The key to acting is using bits and pieces from your real life. Stick with the truth whenever possible—it makes the lies more believable and it's easy to remember the truth, so if you're questioned, you don't have to worry about mixing things up."

Paddy nodded and drew in a breath. "Fishing. There's nothing I love more than heading out for a good day's fishing. I'll even skip Sunday services to go fishing."

"Good job, Fisherman." Dex scanned the papers. "Looks like those Sunday services would be Lutheran. Now, let me tell you about those lovely wife and daughters you left behind in Hamburg."

⊶⊙⊷

AFTER THE SUN abandoned them and there was no sign of Hart or the gray minivan, Drake could stand it no longer. Jimmy in tow, refusing to leave his side, left the federal building and drove over to Alicia Fairstone's historical Shadyside residence. Anyone other than a Fairstone would have called the large colonial on its sprawling lot a mansion, but to Alicia, it was merely her "city house."

Drake barely noticed the elaborate holiday

decorations as he strode up to the front door and leaned on the bell. Alicia had declined an interview when Jimmy had called earlier, directing them to her lawyer instead, but by God, she'd talk to him.

A woman in her fifties opened the door. She wore black stockings and a matronly gray dress. Add an apron and she could have walked straight out of a BBC historical drama.

"We're here to see Ms. Fairstone," Jimmy said. Drake didn't bother with words, simply walked past the woman, barely noticing her expression of outrage.

"You can't—"

He'd been here once before, making final arrangements for *Steadfast*'s sale. Then Alicia had held court in a beautifully appointed salon off the main foyer. He headed that way, leaving Jimmy to deal with any repercussions.

The housekeeper and Jimmy following behind, he crossed into the salon. Alicia was alone, sitting in a chair near the fireplace, reading a book, and sipping from a martini glass. She glanced up at his abrupt arrival.

"Remy. What are you doing here?" She tried to sound surprised, but to Drake it sounded rehearsed. She stood as Jimmy entered along with the housekeeper. Alicia wore a silk pants suit—a lounging outfit the designer probably labeled it—and had her makeup, hair, and jewels ready for a photo op. Staged. That's what the moment felt like.

She'd been expecting him. Or someone.

"You know why I'm here," he said, his tone harsh.

"Ma'am, should I call the authorities?" the housekeeper asked.

Jimmy flashed his badge. "We are the authorities."

Alicia jerked her chin and the housekeeper scurried away. "Would you like a drink?" she offered, resuming her seat.

"How do you know Nickolai Kasanov?" Drake demanded.

"He's a fellow collector. The one who first told me about your work, in fact."

"Kasanov told you about my art?"

"Yes. He emailed me photos of it, along with your bio."

"Bio?"

"That you were a Pittsburgh police detective, pursuing art as a second career. Obviously, with the local connection, I couldn't resist. Especially when he offered to fund half the purchase price with an anonymous donation to the foundation."

"Wait. He sent you my real bio? You knew who I was before—" Drake broke off, the pieces falling into place.

Jimmy and Drake exchanged glances. How the hell had Kasanov manipulated all this? No. Bigger question: why?

Burning *Steadfast,* taking his mother and Hart—this all felt so very personal. Revenge or retribution. Drake had never encountered Kasanov. Yet the man had been planning this for months.

"I don't understand," Alicia said. Again, it sounded rehearsed, not genuine. "I thought you knew Nickolai. He was at the gala last night, didn't you see him there?"

Drake turned to her. "Do you have any idea what Kasanov has done?"

"No. What?" She looked up at him in wide-eyed innocence.

"He kidnapped my mother and fiancée. He's going to kill them, Alicia. And I have no idea why. But I'm guessing you do."

She stood and stepped to him, one hand on his arm in an intimate gesture. "Remy, I wish I could help you, but I don't know anything. I assure you, if I did—"

He shrugged her hand away. She was playing games with him. Was she working with Kasanov? Why? What could Drake have that an heiress and a gangster wanted?

Jimmy's phone rang, shattering the silence. He stood and turned away, speaking only for a moment before returning to hand it to Drake. "It's him."

Drake left Alicia with Jimmy and stepped out into the hall. "Kasanov. What do you want?"

"I see you and Alicia are getting along. Almost as famously as Dr. Hart and myself."

"You touch one hair on her head—"

"Please, Detective. Don't waste what little time she and your mother have left with idle threats."

"Let me speak to them."

"No. I don't think so. Not until you give me something

in return."

"What do you want?"

"Alicia Fairstone. You will deliver her to me by midnight. Dead or alive, I don't really care—although, since you've done your homework and know about my wayward youth, the fun I have with women, I'm sure you'll understand if I'd prefer her alive."

"Why? Why should I give you an innocent woman to torture and kill? Why this elaborate set up? You could have grabbed Alicia yourself any time you wanted."

"Why? Because there's a price to be paid. Alicia must pay the price for her crimes. And you must pay the price for your arrogance and incompetence."

"I have no idea what you're talking about."

"Then I suggest you find out, Detective. Isn't that your job? But know this. If I don't have Alicia in my hands by midnight either Cassandra Hart or your mother will die."

CHAPTER 21

DURING HER SEVENTEEN years of living, Rosa Costello had trusted no more than a handful of men—most of them now dead. She'd been fighting the Nazis for four long years, ever since she escaped the prison camp they'd sent her to after they killed her family.

She was thirteen when she killed her first German—the one who shot her little brother in the face. Chavo was only nine, unarmed, no threat to the mighty military machine of the Reich, but their orders had been to kill any gypsies too young or too old to work, or too capable of fighting back, and to send the rest to serve in a labor camp.

For all their polished boots and sharp salutes, Rosa knew the Nazis were, in their hearts, cowards. Unfortunately, she came to learn as the war became official and countries fell throughout Europe, so were most men.

Which is why this Irishman, this fisherman, this sailor who'd almost drowned until she'd plucked him from the sea's greedy embrace, he intrigued her. Padraic Hart didn't waste her time with stupid questions, yet he didn't follow orders blindly. He was loyal to his men—despite the fact he was no officer—and willing to risk his life for a chance to save theirs.

She listened to him and Dex practice their roles. Dex would switch from friendly banter to mock threats and challenges but the Irishman didn't falter. She smiled. Loyal, brave, and quick-witted. This was a man Rosa could use.

At the outskirts of Bayonne, she pulled the ambulance to the side of the road and joined the men in the rear. It was the dead of night, her favorite time.

She spread several maps over the stretcher and used her torch to illuminate them. "We're here." She pointed to the road. "The security checkpoints we need to get through are here and here. Villa Chagrin is here." She indicated the prison. "We should arrive around three in the morning."

"How do we get in?" Padraic asked. "Climb over the prison walls?"

Dex laughed. "You'd never make it. They have wire at the top of the outside wall and there's a second inner wall that's twelve feet high."

"No. We hit them where they are most weak," Rosa said. "Their people."

"They only have three German guards," Dex

explained. "The rest are Frenchmen."

In the dim light of her torch, Rosa saw illumination fill Padraic's face. "So these," he indicated his uniform, "aren't solely to get us through the checkpoints."

"We go in as if we belong there," Dex said. "Order the removal of our prisoners from the prison hospital. The French won't risk angering the Germans—"

"Or waking them," Rosa put in.

"What if they ask me medical questions? Or to read a patient's chart?"

"Your role isn't to play a doctor. You're an officer on a mission. You want those prisoners. Now."

"*Schnell, schnell,*" Paddy snapped.

"Right," Dex said with approval. "Any medical issues, you delegate to Rosa, Nurse Stein."

"Keep the French busy," Rosa added. "Order them to carry the patients out to the ambulance, to grab their paperwork, all their medications. Don't give them time to think and we'll be in and out again in less than an hour."

"And past the security checks before sun-up."

Padraic scanned the map and nodded. "Where do we meet if things go wrong?"

Dex answered. "We don't. We split up. I'll stay with the ambulance. You make your way to the train station, head south or east. Sooner or later you'll end up in Marseilles."

"And you, Rosa?" She liked the way Padraic looked at her—not challenging her ability, rather with concern.

Dex laughed. "Don't worry about Rosa. They'll never catch her."

Rosa said nothing, merely folded the map and handed it back to Dex, who moved up front to slide into the driver's seat. She grabbed her nurse's satchel, made sure everything she needed was there: bandages, chloroform, scalpels, sutures, Luger pistol. She had two more knives concealed on her body within easy reach.

"You've done this before?" Padraic asked while they sped down the road to Bayonne, their knees jostling together as they perched on the stretchers.

"Yes."

"And it works?"

She smiled. "One thing Germans are good at is following orders. Remember that and it will be fine."

As they approached the first checkpoint, Padraic moved up to take the seat next to Dex, leaving Rosa alone in the back. The sleepy guard never knew it but she had him in the sights of her pistol the entire time. Lucky man waved them through with no more than a cursory glance at their papers.

The next sentry was a bit more punctilious. He actually shone his flashlight in at both Dex and Padraic, but when he saw Padraic's rank, he meekly handed their papers back and asked if they needed him to call ahead to the prison.

"*Nein,*" Dex said as he put the ambulance in gear. "They're expecting us."

Bayonne was hardly the bustling town Marseilles was even in the full light of day, but this time of night, the city was as quiet as any back roads country village. Maybe more so since farmers often rose before the sun.

They approached the prison. Instead of tensing when they stopped at the outer gate, Rosa relaxed, acting exactly as a nurse harried from her bed to retrieve a valuable prisoner would. While the French guard searched the rear of the ambulance, she straightened her uniform jacket, checked her hairpins, then flashed him a disdainful glare when he brushed his hand against her calf.

"Pardon," he muttered. Finding no contraband, he sent them through the gate and directly to the hospital ward.

This was where the Irishman could ruin everything. Until now, Padraic had played his role admirably, being neither too strident and overbearing nor too meek. Instead, he'd acted as if the sentries were simply beneath his notice.

But now the entire plan depended on him. As befitting a German officer, he waited for Dex to come around and open his door. Rosa was already out of the rear of the ambulance, leaving the stretchers behind. Padraic immediately waved two guards over and ordered them to bring the stretchers. They were inside the hospital doors before anyone even asked to see their papers.

"Where are the Englishmen?" Padraic demanded. "They are to be taken for interrogation immediately."

An orderly appeared, his hair rumpled with sleep, uniform crooked. "Which Englishmen, Major?" he asked, smoothing his face with one palm. "We've the pilots shot down two days ago and several sailors brought in just tonight."

Padraic halted, his posture snapping to attention, delivering a glare that made the orderly take a step back. Rosa moved forward. "Do the courtesy of saluting an officer," she told him in a tone that suggested she was saving his career, if not his life. "And if I were you, I wouldn't question his orders."

The orderly straightened and saluted Padraic. He was a Frenchman, so it was an awkward motion, doused in arrogance. Rosa found that trait useful in the French who worked for the Nazis. The collaborators all had a haughty disregard for their countrymen who fought what they felt was a useless war, yet they also despised their German partners. Such ambivalence made it easy to find their weak spots—usually anything that would make their lives easier.

"We have orders for the pilots." Rosa handed the papers to the orderly who relaxed slightly at the routine. "But the Gestapo will also want the others—should we take them all tonight or do you want Major Strauss to make the trip back again tomorrow?" She kept her tone soft as if the decision rested in his hands. Padraic, meanwhile, was prowling the cramped facilities, acting as if he were an inspector general, barking notes to Dex on "infractions."

"Unacceptable," Padraic growled as he came upon a pile of soiled linens left in the hallway. He kicked them aside. "You there. Name?"

The orderly blanched. "Henri Allard, sir, Major Strauss, sir."

"Allard, I will be speaking to your commanding officer." Padraic glanced at his watch. "We are now behind schedule."

"I'm sorry, sir, we'll get the prisoners straight away. Do you have room for them all?"

"We'll make room," Padraic assured him. "Let them have a miserable ride to Paris. It's the last they'll ever be taking."

The orderly chuckled nervously and waved to the guards. Twenty minutes later, the ambulance was packed with two RAF pilots; Lieutenant Carstairs, who was second in command of Padraic's ship; two more junior officers; and three sailors all with a variety of minor injuries. The lieutenant was the worst off. He had a nasty head wound and was unconscious, so he got a stretcher to himself while the rest crowded onto the floor and second stretcher. One of the sailors, a reedy Scotsman named Kerr, perched on the lap of one of the pilots, while Rosa braced against the rear doors where she could watch out the windows.

Dex steered them out of the prison, barely slowing to salute the guard, out of the city, past the first guard post, again with a quick stop, and past the second sentry who was asleep and didn't even see them come or go.

Rosa glanced at her watch. Fifty-two minutes. Mission accomplished. From his place in the front, Padraic twisted around and sought her out across the bodies of the rescued men. He grinned at her, a boyish expression that, despite him being years older than she was, made her roll her eyes and laugh.

"And to think me dear ma said I had no gift beyond working the nets. What do you say, boys, should I see if there's room on a West End stage for me?"

The men howled with laughter, hurling ribald responses about the kind of roles Padraic was best suited for. Rosa turned to watch their rear flank, hiding her smile.

Chapter 22

CASSIE SAW HER chance when one of Kasanov's teenaged thugs rushed through the office door and handed him a phone. He waved Cassie to silence right in the middle of the most exciting part of Rosa and Paddy's hospital escape, got up, and, accompanied by two more of his men, strode out the door. The kids in the office scrambled away, out of sight. Cassie watched through the window as Kasanov kept going past the reception desk and through another door, vanishing.

That left only one guard. He wasn't much taller than Cassie, but had the bulky build of a weight lifter. Not very old, maybe late teens. She was still puzzled by that. Other than the middle-aged lady she'd met at the gallery, the fake psychic, Natasha, they were all very young. Why was that? A way to keep himself at the top of the power pyramid with no one to challenge him?

Vincent had squirreled himself into the shadows behind a large wheeled toolbox similar in size to the crash carts in the ER. He caught her gaze and nodded, holding his knife at the ready. No way was she about to risk a kid's life, but she might not have to.

She squirmed and shifted her weight. "I need to use the bathroom."

It was a tried and tired escape ploy, but had the advantage of being true. The guard frowned at her then looked away as if deciding she was beneath his notice.

"I don't think Mr. Kasanov wants to sit here smelling urine all night," she tried again.

He considered that and stepped forward. He hoisted her onto her feet and shoved her in the direction of the office. She fell sprawling back to her knees.

"Either cut my ankles free or carry me," she told him. She had a glass shard secreted in her fist and could have cut herself free, but she hoped she'd seem more vulnerable, less of a threat, by letting him do it.

Of course, the larger question was then what? As she'd spun her tale for Kasanov, she'd been massaging her legs back to life; she thought she could run. But first she'd need to incapacitate the guard. She had a weapon. Small as it was, the shard was sharp enough to slice flesh down to a major vessel or take out an eye. With her Kempo training and medical knowledge of a body's vulnerabilities, she could kill or maim.

But to take a life? Despite Kasanov's threats, he'd made no move to harm her—in fact, it was obvious he needed her alive until he learned whatever secret from Rosa's past he thought Cassie held.

If this were a movie, the gutsy heroine wouldn't hesitate to slit the nasty guard's throat and make her escape. But Cassie had killed before. With her own hands. Betraying everything she believed in, everything she worked for with every patient she treated.

It had been an act of desperation; the only way to save her and Drake. Deemed justifiable by law, by society, by anyone who heard the story. But not by Cassie. The weight of that act, the final screams that had dwindled to sad whimpers before an infinite silence, these haunted her.

Could she do it again? No, she knew she could—she was physically able. The question was *would* she kill again?

There was no one else's life at stake here except her own. In fact, by escaping, she might be endangering Muriel.

But one thing she knew. She could not stay and allow Kasanov to continue to use Drake's mother as hostage against her. She had to save Muriel.

All this went through her mind faster than the time it took the guard to decide to cut her bonds.

"On your belly," he ordered. Cassie obeyed, rolling over to lay face down on the oil stained concrete floor. The guard planted one foot on the small of her back, pinning her in place, then bent down and pulled her skirt up. There was the click of a knife blade snapping into place. He tugged at the zip ties encircling her ankles and sliced through them.

When he was done, he took hold of her arm and hauled her to her feet. "Don't try anything."

"Thank you." Cassie kept her face lowered and her gait wobbly, pretending that her feet were still numb. She leaned heavily on him, stumbling, as he guided her to the office door. In her peripheral vision, she saw Vincent, as silent as a shadow, move from his hiding place to follow them.

They crossed through the door and she realized the space she'd thought was an office-reception area was actually part of a much larger building. The door Kasanov had disappeared through was across the waiting area and had a window that revealed a wide-open space beyond it. It also had a keypad lock on it as did the door she and the guard had just come through. Which meant she was now trapped in this small section of the building.

A car dealer's showroom? she wondered, straining to see more through the tiny window. But the guard wrenched her in the opposite direction, down a short hall to a small unisex cinderblock bathroom behind the service desk. No windows and it stank as if it hadn't been cleaned in decades.

"Could I have more water, please?" she asked.

"Drink from the sink." He shoved her inside the room and stood in the doorway. "Go on."

She said nothing, merely glanced around the room and then pled silently as she met his gaze. It was obvious there was no escaping from this room barren of everything except the toilet and sink. There wasn't even a paper towel dispenser or toilet paper holder she could rip from the wall and use as a weapon. Just a soggy, tattered roll of paper on the back of the toilet.

The strange staring match continued, Cassie remaining silent and meek, until the guard finally flushed, looked away, and closed the door, giving her privacy. She quickly used the facilities, then ran the water, washing her face and cuts, but mostly drinking as much as possible. Leaving the water running, she pulled the lid off the back of the toilet. It was a better weapon than the glass shard, if not as elegant.

Only problem. She'd get just one shot with it, and it was so bulky that there wasn't enough room to swing it inside the cramped quarters of the bathroom. No way could she smuggle it out of here, so she returned it to the toilet and grabbed her shard of glass.

It was about two inches long, curved on one side, from the heavier base of the bottle, which meant she could hold it without being cut herself. She braced herself and opened the door.

The guard leaned against the wall outside, waiting.

"Thank you," she said, forcing a smile at him.

Again, he looked away, as if embarrassed being caught being kind. She stepped past him then stumbled back as if she'd lost her balance. Instinctively, he caught her before she could fall.

Pushing off with one leg, Cassie pivoted, jabbing her palm up under his chin hard and fast. He cracked his head against the wall he was pinned against. With her other hand, she pressed the sharp edge of the glass against his cheekbone so that if he made the slightest movement it would pierce his eye.

Vincent appeared from the other end of the short hallway. Together they hustled the guard into the bathroom, Cassie exchanging the glass for Vincent's dagger. The guard said nothing—by that time, Cassie had the dagger at his throat—but his expression was murderous.

He had zip ties in his jacket pocket. Vincent quickly hogtied him, then used the man's socks and shoelaces to gag him. Cassie took the guard's knife and pistol—he had no cell phone, unfortunately. They locked the bathroom door from the inside and left, the whole thing had only taken a few minutes.

A rush of adrenalin sparked through Cassie. They'd done it—she was free! Now she just needed to get help, find Muriel, and get them both out of here alive.

Then she realized. She had no idea where "here" was. Or where Muriel was.

CHAPTER 23

Rosa took Paddy and his compatriots to a brothel near Marseille's Vieux-Port. At first, he was nonplussed, but it was the perfect place to hide from Vichy and German eyes. Most of the working girls had fled for more prosperous locales and Rosa had recruited the few who remained into her intelligence-gathering network. Thick drapes blanketed every window, there were hidden tunnels and passages to expedite clandestine exits, and more than enough beds for all. The only thing lacking for the others was fresh air and relief from the boredom brought on by confinement. After three weeks, tempers began to flare.

Paddy, because of his fluency in German and growing competency with the Marseilles French dialect, was the only one able to leave the bordello, accompanied by Rosa, of course. She watched over all of her *"apatrides,"* persons without papers or a country to claim, with the possessiveness of a mother hen. Especially the soldiers. She told Paddy that most of the British Expeditionary Forces stranded in France were at Fort St. Jean, but the city was too mad with fear after news that Vichy's leader, Marshal Petain, was coming for an inspection tour for her to risk moving Paddy's men there.

Each journey outside the walls of the brothel was filled with anxiety and the risk of detection, but the entire city seemed to thrive on cloak-and-dagger machinations. Walking along the cobblestoned streets, watching the reactions of the others who crowded the cafes, gossiping about new routes over the Pyrenees or the cost of counterfeit transit visas, it seemed as if the very air of the port city thrummed with anticipation. The same thrill of anticipation shared by a cornered rat right before a terrier pounced.

People of every social strata clamored for an audience with the "relief" agencies—in actuality small groups of determined men and women who had funds and contacts to help arrange for emigration, either legally or illegally. Mainly Jews, they were of every nationality, out-spoken socialists and communists, artists, writers, scientists, rich, and poor. They shared only one thing in common: they were on the Nazis' list of unwanted. With growing rumors of what was actually happening in the camps to the east, few dared take the chance of turning themselves in when Vichy government decreed it. And so all made their way to border towns like Marseilles where they waited and hid and hoped for salvation.

During the three weeks since Rosa and her group had rescued him and the others, Paddy watched in amazement as this young snippet of a girl calmly and competently organized the exodus of several dozen people across the Pyrenees to freedom. But the German and Vichy crackdowns were taking its toll—two of her groups had to turn back because of heightened border security.

But still, she persevered, finding the means to feed and shelter them and others without funds or papers until she developed a new route.

They were at the Cafe Pelikan, sipping postum, a bitter grain brew that made for a poor substitute for real coffee, when Rosa informed Paddy that she'd be taking him and his men across the border the next day. She even swiped the pepper pot from the table as they left. "Put it in the cuffs of your trousers," she said, slipping it into his coat pocket. "It will keep the dogs off your track."

Later that night, Paddy tossed and turned in his small room papered in fraying brocade and smelling of musk, perfume, and the stale smell of sex. Of course he wanted his men safe, but despite the danger, he didn't want to leave Marseilles. He had tried to express his feelings for Rosa, but each time she had turned him aside, moving the conversation to logistics about his escape.

And why not? He thought with a groan. Who was he

to her? Another mouth to feed, another man who could get her or the people who worked with her killed. After their raid on the hospital to retrieve his fallen colleagues, he thought he'd sensed more from her, but now he realized that all she felt for him was a sense of responsibility.

And all she would feel for him once he was gone would be a sense of relief for another bullet dodged.

He cursed his idiocy and tried to force himself asleep. Tomorrow would be grueling—a ten-hour climb through rough mountain terrain. Their highest ranking officer, Lt. Carstairs, was still not fully back to normal after his head injury. It would be up to Paddy to lead his men to freedom.

The door creaked open and he sat bolt upright, fumbling for the pistol on his bedside table. A flicker of candlelight appeared, followed by a woman's form. The door closed and she advanced. Paddy caught his breath. It was Rosa.

She placed the candle on the washstand beside the bed and stood before him. Her hair was down, framing her face in a cascade of curls. She wore a simple blouse and wool skirt, with a heavy quilt wrapped around her shoulders. In the dim light, she no longer appeared as the formidable resistance leader, La Tempête, but rather as a scared woman-child.

"Is something wrong?" he asked, holding his blankets tightly around his nearly naked body. She stood before him, silent. "What is it, Rosa? You're frightening me."

His words earned him a pensive smile. "You frighten

me."

He blinked in surprise. "I frighten you? How? Why?"

"Your feelings. For me." The smile that crossed her face now had nothing of a child in it, but was all woman. "When you look at me, when your hand brushes mine, I feel—" She broke off, spun around to reach for the candle. "This is a mistake. *Je regret.*"

Oh no, she wasn't getting off that easy. Paddy lunged for the candle, ignored the bedcovers falling away from his body, and grabbed her arm.

"No regrets, no mistakes," he told her, holding her firm, looking into her eyes. She met his gaze, didn't seem to have noticed his lack of clothes. "Other men look at you as I do, other men want you—I've seen you brush them aside without a second glance. Why do I frighten you, Rosa? The truth."

She glared at him, squirmed to get away for one infuriating moment, then drew her breath in. "I have lived with fear for years now—the Germans came after my people long before they went after the Jews. I've been captured…I was frightened, but I escaped. I've almost died, have been forced to face my fear and kill others, and I survive. And by surviving I have been able to keep on fighting against the people who killed my family, everyone I held dear. Even though through this fight, I have earned the wrath and scorn of my own people—that was once my greatest fear, but now," she shrugged, "being cast out as unclean seems—what do you English say? Small potatoes."

"You bloody well know I'm not English, so get to the point. Why are you here?"

Her gaze darted away from his and his breath caught. He remembered how calm she'd been that first night, holding a dagger to Maguire's throat, facing down two dozen angry men, but now she couldn't meet his eyes?

Finally her whisper broke the silence. "You make me afraid—afraid not of capture or death, but afraid of failing. Failing them, you—disappointing you. I'm afraid of wanting more—wanting tomorrow—"

She shook her head, as if words failed her. She knew half a dozen languages, yet she had no words for hope.

The thought ambushed Paddy. He pulled her into his arms, bowed his head over hers as she silently wept, her tears hot against the bare flesh of his chest.

"Rosa, my Rosa. You could never fail me. It's all right to have hope—it's what we all need to make it through this God awful mess of a world with our souls intact. It's all we have, don't forsake it."

She sniffed and looked up at him, her heart-shaped face glowing with wet tears in the candlelight. "*Cat traieste omul spera*, life is hope," she said. "My grandmother used to say that. I never listened. I hated her."

Paddy laughed at that. He hadn't cared much for his gram either. "My gram said the same thing. 'Life is love, love is hope.' Maybe the old hags knew what they were talking about after all."

Her hands skimmed up his bare arms, sending a thrill

through him before coming to rest on the sides of his face. She raised herself up onto tiptoe and he lowered his lips onto hers.

When he woke the next morning, he felt changed forever, ready to face anything. He'd lead his men over the mountains to freedom. And then he would return for Rosa.

Stretching lazily, he reached for her. But the other side of the bed was cold. Before he had the chance to feel regret, the door eased open. It was Rosa, fully dressed, that crazy quilt of hers wrapped around her so she looked more like an old crone than a young girl. It was sodden wet.

"We're not going, are we?" he said when he saw the look on her face.

"No. A storm has moved in. The worst I've ever seen."

Spreading the quilt over a chair near the fire to dry, she didn't turn to face him. "It's worse. Marshal Petain is on his way for his grand inspection. He'll be here tomorrow at the latest. The police are rounding up everyone considered undesirable or dangerous and imprisoning them on a ship, the *Senaia*."

Finally, she turned to him. "They've already raided two of our houses, taken half my people." Her face was ashen. "There's nothing I can do. I've failed them."

Paddy left the bed to gather her into his arms. She wasn't weeping, although her entire body trembled. He wished she would cry, let out some of the pain.

But that wasn't his Rosa. The best he could do for her—the only thing he could do for her—was hold her tight.

CHAPTER 24

DRAKE WAS STILL staring at the phone in his hand when Jimmy joined him out in the hallway. "What did Kasanov want? Were you able to get proof of life?"

"He wants her." Drake nodded toward where Alicia waited inside her salon. "And I have a feeling she knows it."

"Yeah, she's playing this much too cool," Jimmy agreed. "Why hasn't she called her lawyer or the mayor or whoever, fry our asses already? She didn't even seem surprised to see us."

"I need to know what's really going on here. What Kasanov's game really is."

"What did he tell you?"

Drake had an eidetic memory when it came to visuals and his auditory skills were almost as good. He repeated

Kasanov's demands verbatim. Jimmy shook his head as if trying to rattle his brain cells into forging new connections. "You're not giving her to him, of course."

"What makes you so certain?" Drake hated to admit it, not even to Jimmy, but if he thought for one second he could trust Kasanov, he'd sacrifice Alicia in a heartbeat.

"For one, you're not an idiot. You know it's some kind of set-up. For another, either your mom or Hart caught wind of you making a stupid ass move like that, they'd kick your butt from here to Norway and back again."

Drake's lips tightened, but he nodded a grudging agreement. "But now we know it's personal. Something between her and Kasanov."

"And you. Something he thinks you slacked off on—a case?"

"I never worked any case involving the Eastern European mob or Alicia Fairstone. Hell, I never even heard of Alicia until she approached my manager about *Steadfast*."

"Yeah, but what else could it be? Romero is running all your past cases to see if there were any ties to the arson last night. Let's see if throwing Kasanov and Alicia's names into the mix pops something."

"In the meantime, what do we do with her? It's obvious Kasanov's people are watching her."

Jimmy scowled. "I say we arrest her as a material witness and haul her privileged ass down to the station house. With the holiday, no matter how much money she has, no judge will hear her case until Tuesday at the earliest."

"If we're wrong, it's a good chance it will mean our jobs." Drake was perfectly willing to take the risk, but he couldn't let Jimmy. Jimmy had a family to support.

Jimmy didn't even bother answering. Instead, he strode back into the salon and pulled his cuffs out.

⁕

TURNED OUT THEY didn't need the handcuffs. As soon as Jimmy told Alicia they wanted to bring her in for further questioning and would arrest her as a material witness if need be, she seemed almost relieved. Instead of calling her attorney, she'd grabbed a coat and bag and followed them meekly out the door.

The only time she'd appeared at all apprehensive was during the short walk from her front door to the car. Guilty, every cop instinct in Drake's body screamed. But of what?

He felt better once they were safely inside the Zone 7 station house. Not relaxed, but at least able to divest enough of the apprehension that had hijacked his nerves so he could concentrate. Jimmy escorted Alicia to an interview room—he was much better at getting guilty consciences to unburden their secrets than Drake was—while Drake went in search of Romero, the arson investigator.

He found him in the briefing room where they worked major cases. With Romero were Janice Kwon and Don

Burroughs, fellow detectives from Drake's squad. The room lacked the fancy technology the feds boasted but made up for it with dedication. Romero in particular was bleary eyed—he'd clearly been working the case ever since Drake left him earlier this morning.

"Cleared the list you gave me," he greeted Drake. It was better than empty words of sympathy.

Drake looked past him to where Janice was erasing names off a white board. Burroughs worked a computer at the table across from where Romero was surrounded by stacks of paper case files and murder books. "Still can't find any connection between any of your collars and Kasanov."

"Add Alicia Fairstone to the mix," Drake told them. He'd called the feds from the car and had them running their own data search, but some things wouldn't show up in the national databases. "Kasanov called, said Alicia had to pay for a crime—something he blames me for not solving."

"I reviewed your open cases," Kwon said. "There's nothing tied to Kasanov."

Drake knew that. He and Jimmy had one of the best clearance rates in the city; the few cases they hadn't closed were long cold. A John Doe found naked under a bridge with his skull bashed in two years ago. A junkie who'd OD'd of a hotshot delivered by her ex, but the DA said they didn't have enough probable cause to charge the man. A carjacking that had ended with the victim in a coma for the past fourteen months.

Romero looked up from the file he was reading.

"There was one thing I wanted to ask you about. A hit and skip fatality from a few months ago."

Drake remembered the case. "The CMU student? That wasn't my case—belongs to Jo Anderson over at traffic."

"But your name was on a few of the witness statements."

"Sure, I was the on-call detective that weekend, got things started. Then Jimmy and I helped out with the canvass." He nodded to Burroughs. "Don, you were there as well."

"Yep. Poor kid, had all sorts of reflector shit on his bike and still some sonofabitch ran him down. I remember there were no skid marks, no sign the driver stopped at all."

"Jo's team was able to narrow the vehicle's make and model down to Jaguars sold in the past two years," Romero told them.

"Good for her. Did she make an arrest?" Drake asked.

"No. But one of the Jaguar owners she spoke to was—" Shit. "Alicia Fairstone."

"Bingo. No sign she was involved, no damage on her vehicle—but it was days later before anyone got around to talking to her."

Electricity surged around the room as the cops shook off their fatigue and became energized by the lead, no matter how slim.

"Tell me about the victim," Drake said.

"Anton Lavelle, nineteen. Studying computer security. No arrests, no warrants, nothing at all in NCIC."

Drake paced to the white board where Janice wrote Anton's name and particulars in her precise printing. He circled the table and ended standing behind Romero, who was leafing through the case file.

Romero made it to the end of the file that contained all the handwritten notes and other paper detritus that even in this computer age still drove an investigation. "Nothing much here. Lived alone. Friends and professors all said he was a quiet guy, nice, reliable, really smart but not obsessed with anything except school and biking."

Burroughs typed on the computer. "Nothing here either. I'll get Jo Anderson on the line. Maybe there's more that didn't make it into the file."

"Next of kin?" Drake asked

Romero flipped back to the front of the file. "That's weird. None listed. Looks like his emergency contact was his landlady and she made all the funeral arrangements."

Drake frowned, the myriad of pieces swirling through his brain. "Let's see if the feds can make any sense of this." He called Prescott. "Can you run Anton Lavelle? See if there's a connection to Kasanov?"

"Let me give you to Taylor."

Drake gave the FBI agent the particulars, his words punctuated by the sound of keys being tapped at lightning speed. "I'm wondering if this kid is somehow related to Kasanov."

"No sign of it on the surface," Taylor answered. "But you said Anton was studying cyber-security? Maybe we need to dig deeper."

Then it clicked. "You said Kasanov was close to going out of business because he couldn't compete with the mobs who'd turned to cyber-crime. Maybe Anton was his lifeline back to solvency?"

"Looking at the kid's grades, he had the skills. Oh, lookee here," the agent's voice up ticked in excitement. "His high school transcripts are fake. So is his birth certificate. Looks like there's no real record of Anton Lavelle before he came here to start college."

"He had to come from somewhere."

"Not as far as I can tell. I'm running his photo and prints through the Homeland Security facial recognition database—if he came here from another country, we'll find it. Might take some time, though."

Drake stared at the photo of Anton from the file. Not the postmortem one, but the one from his college ID. In his mind he superimposed Nickolai Kasanov's image. Same cheekbones, same cleft chin, same brow line and deep-set eyes.

"I think he might be related to Kasanov. Maybe his grandson?"

"You think Kasanov sent him here to learn the skills necessary to save the family business only to have the kid get killed in a hit and run?"

"I know it's thin, but it's all we've got." Drake paused as Janet Kwon handed him a printout. "The plot thickens. Apparently his landlady—the one who took care of his remains and was listed as his only emergency contact—doesn't exist either."

"Makes sense. If Anton was family, Kasanov would never send him here alone. What's her name?"

"Natasha Mulo, age forty-nine." He gave Taylor the particulars. "Kwon just ran her and can't find anything, like she's a ghost."

"I'll keep working here, but I'm not sure it helps—where's our leverage to use any of this to get your mom and Hart back?"

Drake glanced at the door leading back out to the squad. "Down the hall. I hope."

Chapter 25

Rosa gathered her people, sending as many as she could out to warn her hidden refugees, while she, Paddy, Dex, Fernando, and Matilde, the woman who ran the brothel, gathered in the dining room and tried to prepare for the worst.

Paddy stood on the other side of Rosa as they stared out the window. A police wagon, *panier a salade* Rosa's people called the bowl-shaped vans, passed on the street below, its wheels raising plumes of mud and water so high it was rendered invisible. Rain pelted the windowpanes, mixing with the fog. It was as if the bright and raucous Marseilles he'd come to know had suddenly been transported into a gray, barren dreamscape populated only by ghosts.

The view outside didn't worry him as much as Rosa. Her face and body hidden from the others by the thick drapes, he sensed her dejection and despair as she pressed a hand against the glass.

Behind them the others kept up their funeral dirge, bemoaning their fate alternating with outlandish ideas for escape or protestations of how they'd never be caught alive. Empty words all of it.

The door crashed open and Bernard Lavelle, one of Rosa's lieutenants, ran inside. "They picked up Varian Fry, his entire office staff. Most of his refugees as well."

"All to the *Senaia*?" Fernando, the Basque, asked.

"Loaded up in a *panier a salade* and carted off to the docks." Bernard didn't join the bedraggled group around the table. Instead, he leaned against the still open door. Staring at Rosa, a challenge in his eyes. Paddy was glad Rosa had her back to Bernard, although her posture stiffened as if she felt his gaze.

During his time here, he'd learned that Bernard was a gypsy, like Rosa, but from a different clan. For some reason, that seemed to give the man the idea that he was superior to Rosa. More than that, Barnard often had a possessive attitude about Rosa—Paddy had come across them screaming at each other in their own language, followed by Barnard stalking away after hurling insults at Paddy.

Despite the fact that he was married, it was clear Barnard wanted more from Rosa than she was willing to offer. And that he resented Paddy for gaining her favor.

"I told you," Dex said, his voice filled with false joviality as he reached for the last of the bottle of Armagnac. "When a dictator comes to town, the best thing to do is to flee for the country."

"Any word on when Petain is due to arrive?" Rosa asked, still staring out into the fog.

"No," Bernard answered. "He's coming by private coach, so the train station is in an uproar."

That got her attention. She turned her head to glance over her shoulder at him. "But they haven't stopped the trains?"

He shrugged. "How could they? He might not even arrive for another day."

She nodded even though she was already turned back, focused on the street below. It was empty—no cars, no pedestrians, not even any beggars or street urchins. Eerily silent as the fog rolled in, so thick it was impossible to see the buildings directly across from them.

"Haven't seen a pea soup like this since I left home," Paddy said, more to fill the silence than anything else. "Glad I'm not sailing in it, you'd be blind and lost to the selkies."

He waited for her to ask what a selkie was, hoping to distract her with a story. Instead, she straightened, her hand pressed against the glass curling into a fist. She turned to face him, not just her head, her entire body. Stared at him as if they were the last two people alive on the planet. At that moment, the weight of her gaze on him, he rather wished they were.

Then he spotted the slow smile curling her lips and crinkling her eyes. "You, Padraic Hart," she said in a low tone, "are the most brilliant man I've ever met."

Before he could answer, she whirled to the assembly. Her energy was contagious as they all stirred to life, looking to her for salvation. Paddy marveled at the sight—these men, most battle-tested, all older than her by a half a decade or more, and they didn't think twice about letting her lead.

"Bernard," she ordered, "get back to the station, keep an eye on things there. Anything you can do to increase the chaos, distract the guards and police, do it. Nothing big, just little things that will keep them off-balance."

"You can't be thinking of using your usual route, the train to Toulouse," he protested. "It's too dangerous."

"Maybe not," Dex put in, warming to the idea. "With the prefecture busy rounding up all the undesirables and the guards at the station preparing for Petain's arrival, we might have the window of opportunity we need."

"Go," she told Bernard. "Let us know if you learn more about when Petain is due to arrive."

He frowned but nodded and left. Once he was gone, Rosa joined the others at the table. "Fernando, we need trucks. And a *panier a salade*. Two—no, three of them. Police prefecture uniforms for the drivers."

"Police wagons? Why?"

Rosa didn't take time to answer. Instead she tapped

Matilde on the shoulder. "Take some of the girls down to the docks. I need to know what the procedure is for getting those prisoners onto the *Senaia*. Rounding up so many so fast they probably don't have warrants, but there must be some kind of paperwork, a list, something."

Dex glanced up. "You can't be thinking of trying to rescue the prisoners from the *Senaia*? There must be six hundred or more."

"Oh, there will be more," Rosa assured him with a smile. "I need you to get a message to the British at Fort St. Jean. Tell them to put on civilian clothing and be prepared to be picked up and transported to the docks." She glanced out the window. "The tide. Does anyone know when the tide goes out?"

Padraic couldn't help his burst of laughter. He strode forward to grab her by the waist and swing her around with a glee of delight. "You girl, are a genius."

The men at the table stared at them as if they'd gone mad, all except Dex, who was busy jotting a list onto a scrap of paper.

"More than the tide," Paddy said, feeling like his old self for the first time in weeks. "We'll need to know the tonnage and draft. What kind of engine and navigation—"

"What ships are docked around her and how close," Dex added, catching on.

Paddy nodded. "Charts of the bay would help. We never sailed the Gulf of Lion."

The others suddenly got it. "You can't be serious. Rosa,

are you—?"

Rosa's grin was all the answer anyone needed. "I'm going to steal the *Senaia* and all six hundred prisoners on board."

⚬⟨◉⟩⚬

VINCENT LED THE way back down the hall as he and Cassie left the guard behind. Cassie had taken a folding knife and semi-automatic pistol from the guard; unfortunately, he'd had no cell phone.

"We need to call for help," she whispered to Vincent as they passed the service desk.

"No phones here," he answered. "Only Nickolai's men have them."

Obviously not all of them, which meant grabbing another guard wouldn't necessarily solve the problem. "Do you know where Muriel is?"

He unlocked the door leading back to the service bay and closed it softly again behind them. "Who is Muriel?"

"The older woman Kasanov kidnapped when he took me."

He shook his head, sliding his dagger into his belt and helping himself to a short crowbar. "You came alone. They brought no one else."

Cassie ejected the magazine from the guard's pistol and counted the bullets. Four. Four bullets, two knives, and a crowbar to fight... how many men? She remembered the submachine guns Kasanov's other men wielded.

Outnumbered and outgunned. And she wasn't even sure where Muriel was being held. Which meant Cassie needed to leverage the only advantage she had: Kasanov wanted her alive.

"Natasha and Thomas are still gone," Vincent told her. "Maybe they have your friend?"

They reached the outer door and exited into the night. Goose bumps immediately sprang up over Cassie's bare arms and legs, but she ignored the cold, examining their surroundings. It was an old car lot, turned into a junkyard with abandoned wrecks scattered around towers of smashed cars. Broken glass and metal shone in the moonlight and she realized that with her bare feet and white dress, there was no way she could move quickly or unseen through the maze.

"Are you all family? All these children, they aren't Natasha's, are they?"

"We are family, but not family," he answered. "Natasha, she is our mother. She protects and teaches us, saved us all."

"You're all runaways?" That would explain the older kids—but Vincent appeared to be only twelve or so. "What happened to your parents?"

He shrugged as he led her to shelter behind a school bus that sat up on cinder blocks. "My dad went to jail and Mom just left. They put me in a group home but—" His voice trailed off. "It was bad. So I ran. Found some other kids. Then Natasha came by in her van, fed us, told us about a safe place we could crash, and..."

Cassie didn't press for details. "And Kasanov? Will the other kids do whatever he asks?" She wanted to gauge their loyalty. Could she persuade any of the others to help her?

"Nickolai? He is our protector. No one would dare to not obey him." A shudder shook his thin body as if he just realized what his own act of betrayal might cost him. Then he straightened, his hand going to the hilt of his dagger. "No one except me. I once saw him hit Natasha. He treats her like she's nothing. He pretends to be a good man, but he isn't."

"Do you know where to find a phone?" Her feet were already sore and bloody and they'd only gone maybe twenty yards. She wouldn't make it much farther.

He frowned. "There's a store down the highway. Open twenty-four hours."

"How fast can you run?"

"Very fast," he said, shoulders back, standing proud. "But I'm not leaving you."

"You have to. I need you to run as fast as you can and get to that phone. Call the police, tell them to contact Detective Mickey Drake. Tell them where I am. That they need to come. Can you do that?"

"Of course. But I'm not leaving you." He repeated the last in the same unyielding tone.

"If you stay, they'll kill both of us. If you get help, you'll save us all."

"I'm not afraid to die." He drew his dagger, held it at the ready.

"I know you're not. But we need to save Muriel. You can't let her die. Or the other members of your family. Only you can save them, Vincent."

He considered that. "You'll hide? Stay safe?"

No. But she wasn't about to tell him that. "I'll be fine. Now go. Run fast, as fast as you can."

"For you, my lady, anything." Then he was gone like a shot in the night. Cassie stared after him, wondering how a kid like him had learned chivalry in this world where so many had forgotten the concept. Nice to know heroes were still around.

She sat in the shadow of the bus, flicking stray beads of shattered safety glass from the soles of her feet. She cut a few strips of silk from the dress's underskirt and wrapped her feet with them. Slim protection, but better than nothing.

Now, where to go? She needed to stall, give Vincent time, but her dress practically glowed in the night. However, if she did this right, that might be to her advantage, help her save Muriel. Especially as, if the police got here too soon, if Kasanov had time to make a phone call or transmit a single radio message, it might mean Muriel's death warrant.

Suddenly the yard blazed with light. Men shouted her name. And with them came the sound of dogs barking, howling to be released.

Shit. She wasn't counting on dogs. Shit, shit, shit.

Okay, suddenly hide and seek had turned into a real hunt. With Cassie as the prey.

CHAPTER 26

* ──◆◉◉◉◆── *

"YOUR GRAM," PADDY had told Cassie one afternoon after she and Rosa quarreled and she'd spent the day sulking in silence, "she's a lot like you. Stubborn. Says she don't need nobody." Paddy leaned back against the tree trunk they were sitting under and puffed on his pipe. "She's a good liar. I'll tell you that saved our skins more than once. But she's still a liar."

Cassie had held her breath, not wanting to disturb his reverie, knowing that there was a story coming. Paddy's eyes grew distant as if he himself were traveling back half a century and thousands of miles to a time when ordinary people had to choose between the comfort of compliance and the risk of taking action to save others.

"Was my own damn fault," he began. "Should've never

have let her talk me into the tomfoolery to begin with. Stealing a ship loaded with six hundred refugees right from under the Nazis' noses? While Marshal Petain, the leader of Vichy France, and all his troops were in town, to boot."

He shook his head, tapped his pipe bowl. "But Rosa pulled it off. Saved me and my mates and other soldiers trapped in Marseilles at the same time. We overpowered the guards, skived off in the dead of night, the good Lord sending a nice blanket of mist and fog to cover our escape. It was so bold, so damned audacious, that the Vichy covered it up. One thing you can always count on with the French—their arrogance. No way Petain was gonna slink to his Nazi handlers and ask for help finding us, not after his own special troops had let the *Sinaia* escape—carrying six hundred people on the Nazi's most-wanted list.

"I should have been thrilled as we sped toward Gibraltar and freedom. Here I was having survived shipwreck, encounters with the Vichy and Nazis, and this fisherman from Clifden, a lowly radio operator, enlisted man, was now the captain of a ship, responsible for saving six hundred civilians and thirty-two British soldiers and officers. But it didn't feel right, not having Rosa by my side. And it didn't feel right that I should want her there at all after how angry she made me...."

⟡

Paddy had never in his life thought to meet a woman so

infuriating. Not even a woman. This lass was not yet eighteen, for all her airs of command. Girl thought she was a bloody queen, way she ordered him around! To hell with her. He didn't care if she had saved his life—twice now. Didn't care how many lives she had saved. He was better off without her, damned woman would be the death of him yet!

Rosa Costello would do as she damned well please, just as she always did. The sooner she was out of his life the better. Except it probably would have been easier if he hadn't asked her to marry him—twice now. And if he hadn't kissed her, made love to her. Or if he hadn't fallen in love with her.

"Rosa, come with us, come with me," he'd pleaded before they parted on the dock once he realized the diversion she'd planned meant she'd be staying behind. "For once, let someone else take the risk."

She looked at him as if she no longer spoke English. "I don't understand."

"These people—you've done all you can for them. You know you'll only get caught if you stay here. And they, they don't—" He looked down at his scraped knuckles, unable to break her heart by telling her the truth of how the people she helped viewed her.

"They think I'm a dirty, gypsy whore looking to rob and cheat them."

"You know? Then why? Why stay, put yourself in danger for bigots who are just as bad as the Nazis themselves?"

"They only treat me as *gaje* have always treated my people. The same as my people treat the *gaje*." She shrugged a shoulder. "If I don't save them, who will?"

"Please come with us. Save yourself."

She frowned, seemed ready to trust him with some great secret. Instead, she unwrapped the heavy velvet quilt from around her shoulders and pressed it into his hands. "Take this. Keep it safe for me. There's one more thing I need to do. But I'll join you. Soon. I promise." She stood on tiptoe to kiss him. "I'll find you, Padraic Hart. You can't hide from me, Fisherman."

The sound of dogs baying and men shouting had distracted him. The Vichy searching for the man—Rosa— who'd bombed the customs house. He turned to search the night, gauging how close they were. And dropped his hand from her arm. Just long enough for her to slip free from his embrace and vanish into the shadows.

Now Paddy paced the tiny confines of the *Sinaia*'s wheelhouse, cursing with each step. If he didn't have six hundred-some lives depending on him, he would have dashed after Rosa, stopped her, hauled her back on board kicking and screaming if need be. Even knowing the consequences if he did go after her, he still found his hand on the hatch, had to force himself to step away, return to his post and wait for the signal that they were free of the mooring lines holding them at the dock.

The signal that might announce Rosa's death. His

stomach clutched at the thought and his anger fled. Rosa had out-maneuvered him—again. She'd known exactly what to say to get his temper boiling, to push him away from her exactly when she needed him most.

Not that she'd ever admit any such thing. Stubborn witch. Did he really want to spend the rest of his life with a woman who could make his blood sear, who could outwit him, and who might look like an angel, but who had killed more men in her short life than most of the soldiers on board the *Senaia*?

Alarms blared through the night as search lights cut through the velvet fog that cloaked Marseilles. Gunshots tore the air. Paddy cringed as if they'd slammed into his own flesh. He imagined a too-thin body hurtling to the ground, crimson gushes of blood marring her creamy skin, and blinked back tears.

Dex, looking imposing in his stolen prefecture uniform, appeared in the hatchway. "Lines are cut, we're free."

Paddy nodded, his hands closing over the ship's wheel. "Raise the anchor."

The three words tore through him as painful as bullets. He stared into the night, grateful for the cover of fog, but cursing his inability to see more than glimpses of light and movement on the docks below. The tide was with them; they wouldn't be firing up the engines until they were out of earshot, but they needed Rosa's diversion to last long enough for them to raise anchor—a noisy affair at the best of times.

She had to be alive, he told himself as the lights moved away from the docks and into the narrow alleyways beyond. They're still chasing her. She's alive—please Lord, let's keep it that way?

The wheel shuddered beneath his hands as the *Senaia* slipped free from the docks, past the other ships, and out to sea. The fog closed about her and it was as if she never existed.

A ghost ship ferrying six hundred souls to freedom.

CHAPTER 27

DRAKE FOUND JIMMY standing watch outside the interview room. Beyond the window, inside the tiny room, Alicia Fairstone sat in her lightweight vinyl chair as if it were a throne, appearing strangely relaxed. No one ever relaxed that much in these rooms except for the guilty, relieved the chase was over.

"Did she ask for a lawyer?"

Jimmy shook his head. "Didn't say a word. Just sits there. Like she's waiting for something."

"I think we might have figured out what. Follow my lead." Drake strode into the interview room. "Alicia Fairstone, you have the right to remain silent." He finished reading the Miranda warning to her. Not just for dramatic effect but also because now that he had every intention of arresting her for the hit-and-run murder of Anton Lavelle, or at least questioning her as a suspect. It was required.

Jimmy took his cue and slid one of the standard Miranda forms and a felt tip pen in front of Alicia. "Sign and initial if you understand your rights as my partner has explained them to you."

Alicia didn't move, her gaze briefly flicked to the paper then moved away to focus on the door behind Drake and Jimmy. Not with longing, Drake noted. Rather with relief.

She wanted to be here. Locked up. A few dozen police officers between her and Kasanov.

That alone spoke to her guilt. He thought back to their brief conversation at her house. As soon as he'd told her what Kasanov had done, kidnapping Hart and his mother, everything had changed. He'd been too upset to see it then, but now he understood. Alicia was terrified of what Kasanov might do to her. No wonder she'd surrendered without protest.

Time to see what else she knew. Drake leaned against the table, his back to Alicia but able to watch her from the corner of his eye. He nodded to Jimmy who slouched against the wall beside the door.

"So we've a working theory about the Anton Lavelle homicide," Drake started, talking to Jimmy as if Alicia didn't exist. At his words, a slight tremor shook her calm facade. "You know, the CMU student killed by the hit and run driver a few months ago."

Jimmy had had nothing to do with the case except knocking on a few doors, but he nodded as if he'd been the primary. "Good to know. Poor kid didn't deserve that."

"Yeah, didn't even have any family that we knew of. Just a landlady."

"Until now?"

"Until now. Now the FBI is thinking Anton had ties to organized crime. An Eastern European mob family. Led by Nickolai Kasanov."

Jimmy whistled. "Wouldn't want to be that hit-and-run driver. Not with a guy like Kasanov after me."

Alicia had gone whiter than the walls behind her.

"Unfortunately, we don't have enough to make a case," Drake said mournfully. "Not without a confession."

He and Jimmy shared a comfortable silence. Comfortable for them... hell for any guilty conscience. Alicia leaned forward, her hands clasped tightly on the tabletop. Then she leaned away. Her lips tightened, and for a second, Drake thought they'd lost her. Jimmy gave him the tiniest shake of his head and Drake curbed his impatience.

"I did it," she finally blurted out, the three words filled with the weight of her guilt. "It was me."

"I'm going to pretend I didn't hear that," Drake said, spinning around to face her. "In fact, I'm pretty much deaf to anything you say unless you agree to your Miranda rights and let us start recording this interview properly."

"Wouldn't want the DA to have any questions," Jimmy

put in. "Otherwise, we might just have to release Ms. Fairstone. Send her on her way."

"No, no." Alicia grabbed the Miranda form and scribbled her signature and initials. "No. Please. I want to stay. I want to tell you everything."

"Sure, no problem. Sit tight and we'll take care of you," Jimmy said genially. He and Drake left. Through the window, they watched as Alicia collapsed, crying, head bowed on folded arms.

"Once this is over, she'll lawyer up and accuse us of coercion," Drake said.

"Who cares? We'll get Janice in there with the ADA, they'll do it by the book. On tape." He planted himself against the wall across from Drake. "You're thinking Kasanov got hold of Anton's case file, checked out all the cops involved in the case, and that's why he targeted you?"

Drake nodded. "He somehow found out about my painting and when he realized Alicia was the perpetrator, he put us together, set up everything. I'm guessing with my wedding coming up, it was just too good a chance to use a cop's vulnerability to get what he really wants."

"Alicia." Jimmy frowned. "Which means he doesn't need Hart and your mother. Not alive. Not both of them."

From anyone else, the words would have been cruel. Coming from Jimmy, the truth still hurt—even though Drake had already done the math and come to the same conclusion himself—but it was tempered with the fact that Drake wasn't alone in all this.

Jimmy pushed off the wall. "We'll get them back. Both of them."

"How?" Drake hated asking, but he was out of ideas. "Other than giving Kasanov what he wants?" He glanced at the clock on the wall over the bullpen. Less than three hours left before Kasanov's midnight deadline.

"Not sure yet, but I'm thinking we start by bringing in that landlady, Natasha Mulo. If she's connected to Kasanov, she might have some worth as a bargaining chip."

Drake followed Jimmy back to their desks, suddenly exhausted. One slim hope, that was all they had left. But why would Kasanov keep both Hart and Muriel alive? Killing either one would force Drake's hand, he had to know that.

A red haze filled Drake's mind at the thought that the people he loved were just pawns in Kasanov's quest for vengeance. And there wasn't a goddamn thing he could do about it.

LETTING PADRAIC LEAVE was the hardest thing Rosa had ever done. She'd so desperately wanted to ask him to stay with her, join her in this one last mission. But it was too dangerous and, although she had faith in him, she would not risk his life. Not again.

So, she ran. Hid in the shadows, waiting her chance to distract the police and steer them away from the docks while the *Senaia* and Padraic escaped Marseilles.

She poured all her sorrow and frustration into taunting her pursuers as they harried her through the fog-filled streets. It was almost too easy. A few hours later, the *Senaia* safely away, she returned to the cafe in the hotel beside the Gare St. Charles. Now that Petain had arrived, the trains were running again and she'd had an urgent message to meet her contact from Paris.

"How much gold are we talking about?" she asked him as they both sipped Champagne. Ironic that today was one of the days the government decreed it was forbidden to sell wine or liquor—of course, Champagne counted as neither under French law. One more instance of their passive-aggressive compliance with German rule.

"Eleven kilos," he answered. "A treasure beyond measure. We must ensure its safe passage away from occupied Europe."

"The quickest route would be Paris to Calais to Dover. But the German patrols—" She shook her head. "Not the Channel."

"You'll need help. It's more than you can manage on your own."

With Padraic and the others gone, there was nothing keeping her here. "I'll join you in Paris. We'll find another route."

He glanced at his watch. "My train back will be boarding shortly. Contact me when you're ready."

He left money on the table, more than enough to cover

the bill. She sorted through the coins, glancing around the cafe to make sure he wasn't watched or followed. Then she rose to leave. As she turned, her gaze snagged on a familiar man hunched over the bar where he was observing her in the mirror. Bernard. What was he doing here? How much had he heard?

She made no sign she'd recognized him and left by the front door instead of her usual route through the secret door that connected the cafe to the train station—she couldn't compromise her Parisian contact. Walking fast but with her head held high as if she was in no rush at all, she crossed the street and darted down a narrow alley. The fog and rain were finally thinning. She cursed her luck. Another hour of cover would have been nice.

Footsteps sounded behind her. Then a man called her name. Bernard. When they'd first met, she hadn't trusted him. He was Lowara, a clan that often sparred with hers, and what little she could discover about the events that had led to her family's massacre at the hands of the Nazis suggested that they'd been betrayed by a fellow Rom. But Bernard had proven his worth time and again.

Why did she feel so apprehensive now? Was it because she'd sent her best people with Padraic on the *Senaia*? She'd never minded working alone before.

Maybe it was heartache over Padraic leaving. If so, then best get on with her work, faster to heal any wound if you kept your mind off the pain.

Bernard called again. "Rosa, are you all right? I heard

gunshots down at the docks but by the time I arrived you were nowhere to be found."

She slowed her steps. Stopped and turned to face him. "I'm fine."

"Did they escape?" He drew close, his face flushed from chasing her.

Again she felt that flutter of anxiety, pushed it away. "Yes. Thank you. Your diversions at the station were a huge help."

He gave her a small bow. Stepped forward so that only a foot separated them. "I couldn't help but overhear. What is this new treasure? This gold? Can we use it to fight the Nazis? Are you smuggling it out to De Gaulle? How can I help?"

Rosa narrowed her eyes, one hand sliding to her knife. Too many questions. And that gleam in his eye. "Not here. I'll tell you when we get back to the Rue Royale. We'd best take different routes."

He took her arm in his. "No need. A young couple walking together will attract less attention."

He was right—it was exactly the reason she gave her people when she took Padraic out with her on the streets. She wished now she'd dared to admit the real truth to anyone, herself included.

She allowed Bernard to guide her down to the mouth of the alley, back onto the street. With the rain slowing and the earlier police outcry died down, people were coming out again, returning to their normal routines before the disruption of Marshal Petain's arrival.

Still, Rosa did not move her hand away from her dagger's hilt. She sensed tension in Bernard. Maybe it was the thrill of eluding the police, maybe it was the excitement of a new mission, maybe it was something else.

A man's footsteps dogged their path, but it was a busy street, nothing too remarkable about that. Then a second man. Rosa twisted free of Bernard's arm. "Run," she told him.

He stopped, his expression one of surprise. She sprinted around the next corner even as she shrugged out of her overcoat and tied her hair back with her scarf. Suddenly transformed from a respectable woman to a ragged gypsy beggar girl, she slowed to a walk and crossed the street.

Too late. A *panier a salade* sped toward her. She turned to bolt down an alley but two policemen were already there, pistols drawn. Pointed at her.

Chapter 28

Cassie scrambled across the scrap yard filled with the skeletons of cannibalized vehicles. The dogs' barking echoed through the night, but they sounded as if they were getting close. Climb, she had to get to high ground where she'd have the advantage.

She spotted a large piece of equipment similar to a crane but that had a large metal disk hanging from its derrick instead of a hook. The magnet used to lift the heavy vehicles. Perfect.

The layers of silk she'd wrapped her feet in had shredded to nothing and she felt every stone, every discarded shard of metal as she ran. She forced herself to focus on the magnet. If she reached that, she would be safe from the dogs, and right now that was all she could think about. That and the sight of all the gruesome maulings and dog bites she'd ever treated.

There was a reason she was a cat person. Rosa had hated dogs, said the Nazis used them to torment prisoners. Had talked as if it were a personal experience. Said it wasn't the poor creatures' fault, it was the men who'd trained them, but still, she just wouldn't have them in the house.

Cassie's breath quickened at the thought and she had to force herself to remember her Kempo training and regain control. Center yourself, she thought. Just like sparring. You have a plan, make it work.

Dodging around another stack of flattened cars, she saw the magnet ahead. The dogs sounded as if they'd surrounded her, were closing the net, coming in for the kill.

She clipped the folding knife she'd stolen from the guard into the bodice of her dress. No pockets meant no choice but to keep hold of the pistol as she climbed. She shot forward with one last burst of speed, ignoring the pain in her feet, and lunged for the ladder leading to the magnet's control box. The box was like a truck cab but much higher in the air and enclosed with glass, giving it a good view of the magnet as it swung its heavy and potentially lethal loads. If she could get inside, she'd be protected from the dogs.

If it was unlocked. Perched on the small platform at the top of the ladder, she yanked on the door handle, locked. She peered through the window, tried to see if there was another way inside. Nothing.

The first dog arrived below her, lunging at the lower part of the cab, leaping as high as possible, its jaws snapping in the air below her feet. Close, too close. She inched around to the backside of the cab, away from the dog. The derrick holding the magnet joined the cab here.

It wasn't designed to be climbed like a ladder, the rungs were spaced too far apart, but it was possible. The only hope she had of reaching high ground. Another dog joined the first, racing back and forth at the bottom of the magnet, growling and barking in frustration.

She swung one arm onto the nearest horizontal support and hauled her body up the derrick. As she climbed, the dogs' handlers joined them, throwing swaths of bright light up at her.

"Come down," one shouted. "There's nowhere to go."

Wrapping her arm around one of the vertical supports, she swung to face her pursuers, her pistol aimed at them. Two men were scrambling up the ladder leading to the cab. She shot out the window inches above their hands. "Stop! The next one hits your head."

It was a futile gesture and they all knew it. They could easily out wait her and they had more ammunition than she had. Not to mention more men to out flank her.

But she wasn't planning to stay up here all night. She just needed to give Vincent enough time to escape. How long had it been?

The men below seemed in no rush—in fact, they had

leapt off the ladder and were now laughing at her. She was certain she was a sight they'd never seen before: barefoot in a billowing white wedding gown, hanging off the side of a derrick, aiming a pistol at them. If she wasn't gambling with Muriel's life, she might have laughed herself.

As it was, she was closer to crying. Especially as their high-powered flashlights caught the black streaks of grime and blood that stained Muriel's poor dress. There were so many more important things she should be worried about: had Vincent made it to the phone yet, was Muriel still alive, could she reason with Kasanov?

But still, she couldn't stop a gush of tears at the sight of Muriel's dress, her gift to Cassie. Awkwardly, she ducked her face into the crook of her shoulder, wiping her tears so she could see clearly. Time to bargain.

"Come down," one of the teens called up. Several others were circling around to the other side of the magnet. Cassie whirled on her perch, one foot slipping free, dangling in the air until she was able to find purchase on the metal run once more. She aimed her pistol at the new threat.

"Tell them to stop. I want to speak with Kasanov."

"No, you don't. He's really pissed off at you. Says your friend will pay dearly."

"If he hurts her," Cassie gulped, hoped her bluff would work, "tell him he'll never get the gold. Tell him, if he doesn't let Muriel go, I'll kill myself."

She raised the pistol to her temple. The men took a

step back. Even the dogs quieted. The only sound she heard was the rustle of silk against metal.

The scrapyard spread out below her like an alien landscape. As alien as the thought of pulling the trigger.

Would Kasanov call her bluff? Or would he free Muriel?

Chapter 29

⊹ ❈❖❈ ⊹

The idiot Brits on Gibraltar had been both astounded and flabbergasted by the arrival of the *Senaia* and the stories it brought with it. An Irish seaman, a handful of his fellow shipmates, another two dozen soldiers from the British Expeditionary Forces, and six hundred civilians, including some of the greatest scientific and artistic minds of Germany, all saved by one seventeen-year-old girl and her rag-tag group of Maquis? Preposterous.

"Our man in Lisbon has a working arrangement with a leader, code name Tempest," Archer, the MI-9 official who was debriefing Paddy, insisted. "Right now, he's preparing an escape route for six RAF officers over the Pyrenees."

Paddy was tired of arguing with Archer. He was

exhausted and his temper wearing thin. "La Tempête is Rosa Costello. Without her, your men and future escapes from the south of France are in danger. You have to let me return."

The only reason Archer was willing to listen to Paddy's request that he be seconded to Intelligence instead of returning to his billet as radio operator on one of His Majesty's warships, was that Paddy agreed to reveal the inner workings of Rosa's network, promised that if they let him save Rosa, then the Brits could use Rosa and her people.

Rosa would kill him for betraying her confidence—her passion for secrecy was the only thing that had kept her alive this long—but Paddy didn't care. Not if it gave him a chance to find her again.

"Look here, good man," Archer said in his infuriating Eton accent. "We do know what we're doing—"

"Then who's Fisherman? Tempest's newest radio operator, do you know his identity?"

Archer cleared his throat. "Not exactly. You see, our man in Lisbon was killed in a car accident, everything burned with him. But Fisherman must have been compromised because Tempest himself contacted us about retrieving our men. Unusual, because in the past, he'd always maintained his distance from radio communications."

Paddy shook his head, tried not to laugh. "Fisherman wasn't compromised. He's standing here before you. And you're right, Rosa never used the radio herself—too risky. Whoever contacted you must be working for the Krauts."

The other man's face blanched. "If what you say is true, then we almost released the position of those RAF officers—"

"To the bloody Nazis." Paddy considered his options. "Ask your people if they've received any information on Rosa Costello's whereabouts. She most likely was captured, maybe killed, the night we sailed. Give me that information and I'll go back, save your people."

"They're your people too," Archer snapped. "You are still a subject of His Majesty, the King."

"Ah, but I'm a lowly merchant sailor. Not even an officer. What do I care about some RAF flyboy? Unless of course, I was seconded to Intelligence."

Archer narrowed his eyes but picked up his phone. About bloody time. Paddy tried to sit still, but after listening to a few minutes of "civilized" chatter that had nothing to do with anything important, he could contain himself no longer and began to pace the elegantly appointed office. Not even the view of the Mediterranean could calm him, even though all his life the sea had been his refuge. The thought of learning Rosa's fate pushed all that aside.

Finally, a tall blond man with a hawkish nose and linen suit entered the office, depositing a folder on Archer's desk. He cleared his throat and wiped his hands with his handkerchief as if the contents of the file were distasteful.

Paddy wanted to rip the papers from Archer's hands, but instead stood at attention across the desk. Archer looked up, a frown on his face.

"You never said that this Costello woman was a gypsy. She's not even French. She's *apatrides*, a person without a country or passport."

"What happened to her? Is she still alive?"

Archer didn't answer his question right away, instead looked past Paddy as if he were invisible. Paddy felt his hopes sink into despair.

"It appears we have made a miscalculation," Archer began.

"Miscalculation? What the bloody hell does that mean?"

"We thought she was, uh, entertainment for the Gestapo officers," Hawknose put in. "It wasn't until we debriefed Lieutenant Carstairs that we learned differently."

Paddy narrowed his eyes. "Because she was a gypsy and a woman you assumed she was a whore? That's why you wouldn't believe me, Irish bastard that I am—"

"Now, Hart, there's no call for—"

"Just tell me she's alive, goddamn it!"

Paddy's words echoed through the vaulted ceilinged room. Hawknose took a step back as if fearing violence while Archer spread his hands in surrender. "She's alive. As far as we know," he qualified. "It's difficult to obtain accurate—"

"Where, damn it?"

"Paris. The Fresnes Prison, best we can tell."

Paddy staggered back a step and sank into the chair behind him. Oh god, Rosa. In Marseilles, he'd heard the horror stories emanating from Fresnes. The Gestapo had turned it into their own chamber of horrors where they kept prisoners for interrogation—torture was a better word—before sending them east to an extermination camp.

"I'm sorry, Hart. There's nothing we can do."

"Send me back. I can save her."

Archer looked up at that, his previous look of haughty superiority now replaced with pity. "No one can save her—she's in the belly of the beast, man. There's nothing you or anyone can do. But we need to re-establish an escape network in the south of France. Do you think you can tackle the job? It would take me weeks to get anyone else trained and ready and we've men desperate to escape. Are you up it?"

Paddy rose to his feet and looked down on the official who saw the war as a chess game, his pieces sliding about on a board and bearing no resemblance to men and women with hearts and loves and fear and courage. He wanted to spit on the Brit with his manners and polish, but he couldn't—Rosa needed him. These bloody fools weren't going to save her.

So instead, he fisted his hands at his sides and nodded. "When do I leave?"

⁂

THIS TIME KASANOV'S call came on Drake's cell. Drake and Jimmy stepped into the Commander's office where they could have some privacy. Arrogant bastard knew the FBI would be monitoring it, but he didn't care.

Drake answered, putting it on speaker. "I've done what you wanted. Alicia Fairstone is being arrested for the murder of Anton Lavelle. She's going to lose everything: her social standing, her reputation, will probably spend the rest of her life in prison. Now let my mother and Hart go."

"That's not what I asked for," came Kasanov's measured reply. "I want her life in my hands. Just as my grandson's life was in hers. I want her to see my face as she dies, just as my grandson saw hers."

"You know I can't do that. Besides, dying is too easy, too quick. Too private. A woman like Alicia, public humiliation is the ultimate torture." Drake held his breath, waiting for Kasanov's reply. Hoped he'd played the psychopath correctly. A man like Kasanov... who knew?

"Maybe. Still, I asked for a woman's life and that's not what you delivered. Hardly worth two lives in return, now is it, Detective Drake?"

"It's the best you're going to get. Release Hart and my mother and you'll have a chance to get away before the FBI finds you."

"Do you really think I care about the FBI? Or even escaping with my life? This is about family, Detective Drake. This is about securing a future. You and me, we are meaningless."

Drake blinked in surprise. Psychopaths only cared about themselves, about gratifying their own twisted needs. What kind of game was Kasanov playing?

"Then let my family go." The words came out choppy as Drake tried and failed to keep his emotion out of them.

Kasanov laughed. "I'll let one go. You choose. Your mother or Dr. Hart?"

"You sonofabitch—"

"You have ten seconds, Detective Drake. Who will go free?"

"I can't—" Drake's fist closed so tight around the phone he thought he might crack it. Or hurl it across the room in frustration. Jimmy stepped closer, but Drake waved him off.

"Your mother or Dr. Hart?" Kasanov's voice was calm, clinical. As if the choice were obvious.

Jimmy scribbled a note and held it up for Drake. *Don't play his games. Hang up.*

Drake squeezed his eyes shut, considered it. But no way could he take the chance that they'd lose Kasanov—and with him both Hart and Muriel.

Hart's face filled his vision. He knew what she would want, what she would tell him to do. It didn't make it any easier.

"Time's up, Detective Drake. Who will it be?"

"My mother." The words emerged strangled and twisted with pain. "Let my mother go."

"Very well. We'll be in touch. I'll say good-bye to Dr. Hart for you."

Kasanov hung up.

Drake's entire body trembled with rage as he stared down at the now blank screen. What had he done?

Chapter 30

Despite Paddy's pleading, the Brits gave him nothing to do as they planned his journey back into occupied France except to sit on his bum and dream of Rosa and what might be happening to her.

As he tossed and turned later that night, try as he might, he couldn't banish the image of her face, flushed with emotion, when he last saw her. He'd thought she was angry with him, now he realized it was fear that had colored her features. And yet, still she'd gone, raced through the night into the arms of the enemy.

For the sake of six hundred strangers. For Paddy.

He stifled a groan and took another sip of the Laphroaig he'd stolen from Archer's cabinet. Not as smooth as Jamieson, but it would do in a pinch. Bloody poms sitting here in the lap of luxury compared to what their brethren in Europe or back home had. The war was a game to them, played long-distance; they had no idea what real war meant. He doubted if Archer or any of his staff had ever had a ship torpedoed out from under them, ever been shot at, ever had to run and hide for their lives.

And these were the men the world was relying upon to stop the bloody Krauts and their madman, Hitler?

That thought called for another drink. Slowly the whiskey wound its way through his frazzled and frayed nerves, finally allowing him to sleep. In his dreams, he relived the night he and Rosa had—their one and only night. It was only five days ago, but a thousand years could pass and he would never forget it.

The bittersweet memory lulled him to sleep, tears warming his cheeks.

⁂

DRAKE AND JIMMY took turns pacing the Commander's office. The Commander herself, along with their fellow detectives, worked what little leads they had out in the bullpen, occasionally poking their heads into the office and offering what reassurance they could.

Bottom line, no one could find Natasha Mulo or even any trace that she or Anton Lavelle had existed before their arrival in Pittsburgh five months ago. More interestingly, it appeared Anton's death might not be totally accidental.

Alicia's account of the hit-and-run was that Anton was already down, he and his bike sprawled on the ground, when she rounded the blind corner and ran over him.

Before Drake had time to process that information— had someone discovered Anton's connection with Kasanov and targeted him?—his phone rang.

"There's a package waiting for you," came a man's voice. Not Kasanov. "The Coretti warehouse in the strip district."

"Let me talk to Hart." His only answer was the sound of a dial tone. "Son of a bitch!" He threw the phone across the room, almost hitting Jimmy as he came through the door. "Let's roll," Drake said, moving past Jimmy.

Jimmy grabbed the cell phone and grimly followed his partner.

They phoned Prescott and had dispatch send radio cars, but with Drake driving the streets like it was LeMans, not Pittsburgh, he and Jimmy pulled up at the same time as the first RMP. Abandoning standard reconnaissance protocol, Drake was out, sprinting toward the warehouse before Jimmy could stop him.

The door to the warehouse stood open, an invitation to catastrophe. Drake hesitated only long enough to grab his flashlight from his coat pocket and then he was through it, Jimmy on his heels. They both quickly rolled out of the light of the door, ending up on the right hand side of the dark, cavernous space.

Keeping their back to the wall, they duck walked

along the wall for a few feet until they were surrounded by darkness. The uniforms came in behind them, circling in the opposite direction. Drake tapped Jimmy's arm and then turned the powerful flashlight on, quickly aiming it through the space in front and to the side of them.

Drake's finger tightened on his service piece when the pale flesh tones of a mannequin were illuminated, but he held his fire. The warehouse floor was littered with dozens of the dress dummies, all naked, leering at the two police officers with their plastic smiles.

A pigeon flew up, breaking the silence and sending Drake's heart lurching into a tailspin. He kept scanning the room until he found the electric box on the near wall. He covered Jimmy as Jimmy crept forward and flipped the breaker on.

The overhead lights illuminated a macabre holiday affair. Besides the dummies, there were props for various seasonal displays. Uncle Sam in full red, white, and blue regalia towered over two bunnies carrying Easter baskets. An old-fashioned Saint Nicholas trailing a sled of presents stood beside them.

And tied to an I-beam with duct tape and silver tinsel was Muriel Drake.

CHAPTER 31

CASSIE HAD NO idea how long she clung to the derrick, but it was long enough for her teeth to start clacking together with the cold. Several times she had to shift position so she could hug her gun hand close to her body and keep it warm enough that she didn't drop the damn thing.

Kasanov remained inside but the children and three of his teenaged goons encircled the base of the magnet, jeering at Cassie, rough housing with the dogs, even building a fire, as if this were a party. The children acted almost feral, didn't seem to understand there were lives at stake.

One of the teenagers—the oldest, maybe nineteen or twenty—had a cell phone. He got a call then held it up to Cassie. "Can you see? Your friend and Drake, walking away, unharmed."

She was too far away to see it, but sooner or later she had to climb down and she hoped she'd given Vincent enough time to alert the police. From her view up on the derrick, she couldn't see any lights from cars or buildings, so she feared that the highway and store he'd gone to were farther away than she'd thought.

"Throw down your gun," the kid ordered. The others came alert, the ones with guns aiming them at Cassie, the younger ones scampering around and calling her name in a singsong as if they were playing Red Rover.

Cassie hated guns—had seen too many traumas resulting from them in the ER—but Drake had insisted she learn how to handle one properly. Turned out she was actually a pretty good shot and, although she'd never admit it to him, she enjoyed shooting at the range with him. She released the magazine and dropped it down to the men below, made sure the chamber was also empty, then threw the unloaded pistol down.

"Now, come on down. Don't keep Nickolai waiting."

She swung onto the ladder, one hand sliding the folding knife deeper into her bodice where she hoped it would remain hidden. Teeth chattering from the cold and her feet numb, slipping on the rungs, she climbed down. All she had to do now was stay alive long enough for Drake and the police to get here. *If* Vincent had made it out.

He wasn't among the group waiting for her on the ground. She stopped on the side of the magnet's control cab. "No dogs."

The boys laughed at that, but two of them pulled the dogs back by their collars and held them. She climbed down the rest of the way and stood, hands open at her sides, posing no threat. "Take me to Kasanov. I'll tell him everything."

Everything she knew, that was. Which was pretty much nothing Kasanov wanted to hear.

Time to see if any of Paddy's talent for storytelling had passed down to Cassie.

◦◦◦

ROSA WOKE TO the sounds of a woman screaming. *Lashav,* she chided herself. Shame. Because she could not deny her relief that the screams were not her own.

She wrapped her arms around her body, shivering in the chill air of the unheated room, rolled over, and huddled in a ball. She almost preferred the barren environs of her cell back in Fresnes to being confined here in the excessively opulent hotel on the rue des Saussaies. The Gestapo leadership had commandeered the hotel both for their living quarters as well as their "special" interrogations, calling it their *Gasthaus.*

The cold tile floor of the lavatory that comprised her prison gave her little comfort. Often she would awaken to find one side of her body numb and etched with the fleur-de-lis pattern inscribed on the tiles. Her jailers laughed at a gypsy like her being forced to sleep inside one of the most luxurious hotels in Paris.

They slept in the bedroom beyond with silk sheets and thick duvets. They delighted in bringing their food in on silver-plated trays, the smell of braised beef overwhelming as it perfumed the air, and eating in front of her, purposely dropping crumbs to the ground, just out of her reach from where she sat, her ankle chained to the bidet, letting the food rot as her empty stomach gnawed itself.

She kept telling herself food would do her no good. As soon as they finished their meals and began to question her, she would inevitably vomit. One of the many messy side effects of near-drowning. Hence the lavatory as her prison cell. All the easier to fill the bath tub with icy water and dunk her into it, never knowing if this was the last time, the time they would miscalculate and hold her under too long.

Her grandmother had predicted Rosa would die in the water. Now she knew it to be true.

Rosa tried not to waste precious energy in crying. She was stronger than that, better than that. She was Kalderasha.

But the tears came anyway. Her only comfort was that she had yet to tell them anything—anything they could understand at any rate. She'd confined herself to speaking Romani, the gypsy language few outsiders understood. Another thing Grandmother always said, *"tshatshimo Romani,"* the truth is in Romani, not the ugly *gaje* tongues.

That thought made her feel better. That and knowing that the longer she hung on, the longer she gave Padraic and the others time to escape to safe harbor. What day was it now? She'd lost track after the first few days—days punctuated by beatings by the prefecture followed by beatings by Patin's private guard, then a bumpy ride in a *panier a salade*, followed by more beatings at the Fresnes prison once they arrived.

Back in Marseilles, after that bastard Bernard betrayed her to the police, they had almost let her go as a mistake when she cursed and shouted at them, the image of a crazed gypsy, a *ziegeuner*. Her people were often reputed to be half-wits and feeble-minded, so Rosa used their preconceptions against them. Plus, she'd noted that the Germans hated dealing with unpredictable quantities in their prisoners. Even if they did arrest her, usually they'd send someone acting crazy to St. Cyprien, one of the camps south of Montpelier.

Perfect. From there she could escape and be back in business within a few weeks. A little holiday in the country. She deserved it after all her hard work. Not to mention the beatings she had endured in the name of resistance.

The only thing she would miss would be Padraic. God, the man was infuriating, the way he'd wormed himself into her mind, into her heart. She was glad she had slept with him—glad she had chosen him to be her first. Maybe her only the way things were going. But that night he had been gentle, patient with her in a way totally unexpected, as if he cherished her, as if she were precious to him. She had slept in his arms afterward, her first full night of uninterrupted sleep in years. He had earned her trust, her fisherman. And so to him, she had entrusted the fate of her *apatrides*.

But then, just as she was about to skive free of the befuddled local police, Petain's private guards came. Along with Bernard, who denounced her as the leader of the plot to steal the *Sinaia,* as the one all of Vichy had searched for, for so long, La Tempête.

They quickly subdued and disarmed her, placing her in manacles. Despite the iron that bound her, she had stormed Barnard, knocked him off his feet, and tried her best to strangle him with her chains. It took three guards to haul her off the bastard.

Bernard had sat up in stunned amazement, his hand rubbing his bruised neck as the guards beat her into submission. She lay on the ground, hands now chained behind her as the guards manacled her feet as well, when Bernard knelt beside her, his face lowered to hers.

"Do not fear for your charges, Rosa," he whispered in a hoarse rasp. "I have found your radio. I will take care of everything for you. And if we find your *gaje* lover, we'll take care of him as well."

Rosa spat in his face. He stood and kicked her in the head so hard that she blacked out. When she came to, she was face-down in the back of a police wagon, alone in the dark.

Just like now. She wished the lavatory had a window so she could tell if it was day or night. Even just to see a glimpse of the sky—she'd like to see the sky one last time before she died.

She had a feeling that might be today. The Gestapo major who led her interrogations was getting bored with his little games—the dunkings, the beatings, the hauling her up to hang by her arms until her shoulders felt as if they would burst free of her skin and her chest grew so tight she could not breathe. She knew soon her stubborn silence would drive him to push her further.

She also knew what he didn't know. That she wanted him to lose control, to go too far, end this for good. That her strength had fled from her a long time back. Now she was only hanging on because of sheer panic that if she caved, it would mean death for Padraic and the six hundred she had placed in his care.

Life is hope.

Her grandmother's words came again. Why was it, as she lay here on the floor beside a filthy toilet, near to death, that she couldn't get the old bitch out of her head? Her grandmother had been a mean-spirited woman who never raised a hand to do more than order the younger members of her family, particularly her daughter-in-laws, around. She had harangued them all, disparaging their looks, their abilities, their work habits.

Rosa had despised the woman, vowed never to be like her when she grew older.

Maybe she was already dead? Maybe that was why her grandmother's ghost seemed so near right now?

A cramp spiraled through her side when she took a

breath. She coughed; more agony shot through her ribs and lungs. No, not dead yet, Grandmother—you'll just have to wait, you old haint.

The coughing spell left her gasping. She spit out a wad of mucus that was certain to be blood streaked. She shivered and knew it was from more than the cold. She had a fever, pneumonia no doubt from the repeated near-drowning. She must have swallowed half the Seine these past few days.

The door opened and light flooded the small room, blinding Rosa. She squinted her eyes, able to focus only on a pair of spit-polished black boots. Their owner stood above her; she didn't bother to waste energy in lifting her head to stare up at him. *Here we go again. Won't be long now, Grandmother.*

The officer shouted in German, not the voice of the Major who was her usual inquisitor. She heard thumps as her guards hastily thrashed into their own uniforms and boots. Still night, then. What would bring an officer to her at night? Especially an officer high-ranking enough to intimidate her guards?

Maybe they had given up on her, were giving her to the officer as a plaything, a sex toy to whet his perverted appetites? She'd heard of such things, but thought the Germans were too meticulous to stoop to the level their Vichy compatriots were rumored to. Her own guards seemed repulsed by the thought of touching her at all, had worn leather gloves any time they handled her as if they might be contaminated by an inferior specimen of humanity such as Rosa.

Then Rosa heard the name that struck fear into her heart. Karl Bömelburg. The Director. In charge of Gestapo operations in all of France. Bömelburg was the monster the Gestapo major had threatened her with, gleefully describing in painstaking detail how he'd broken even the strongest resistors.

Rosa curled into a tighter ball, her body shivering uncontrollably. Bömelburg barked out more orders and Rosa's guards hustled into the lavatory, hauling her to her feet and holding her there while they unlocked her chains. She sagged in their arms, her bare feet barely touching the floor as they dragged her out into the night, wearing only her stained and torn shift, following Bömelburg to a waiting Citroën.

She could tell the man was used to being in command by the way he carried himself, haughty, superior. Even though she could only see the back of his uniform, she had a good idea of the type of man Bömelburg was. For the first time in days, she felt truly afraid. Drifting into the quiet death offered by drowning was far different from anything this man might have planned for her.

Her guards threw her into the back of the staff car, they were so anxious to snap to attention and salute the great man, Bömelburg. Rosa bounced onto the seat, landed face-down. The front passenger door opened and closed, followed by the driver's side door. They sped into the night, leaving Paris behind.

There was a closed partition between the driver and passenger compartment. All Rosa heard was the deep purr of the well-tuned engine and the occasional muttering of her new captors. They stopped several times at guard posts, but not long enough for the driver to do more than pause.

Of course. No one wanted to annoy the great Karl Bömelburg. Especially when he was in possession of a new plaything: Rosa.

She fell into an oblivious stupor until, finally, they pulled off the main highway and onto a rutted lane that strained even the Citroën's superior suspension. Every bounce cut through Rosa like a knife, but she kept quiet in the dim hopes that her captors had forgotten her. Then they rolled to a stop.

The door opened and hands reached in and slid her free of the back seat with a gentleness that surprised her. She was lowered to the ground onto a blanket that was then wrapped around her. In her confused state, she could have sworn the blanket was her own perina, the one she had entrusted to Padraic.

It was total darkness, not even stars could be seen, only the glowering shadows of the two men above her. They were in the woods. She could hear the rustle of tree branches, smelled decayed leaves.

The car sped away into the darkness, leaving one man behind—Bömelburg, she could tell by his build. Was he going to kill her here and now? No, not so fast. Bömelburg was known as a man who enjoyed prolonging his pleasure and the misery of others.

A faint moan escaped her as he knelt beside her, pulled her into his arms. She felt his breathing coming in choked gasps, smelled the tang of his sweat through the heavy wool clothes that swathed him.

Rosa felt a stir of hope. Maybe she was already dead? Or dreaming?

She raised a hand to his face, her fingers tracing the contours of his jaw and cheek, sliding against silent tears that slid from his eyes.

He drew his breath in with a ragged gasp and held her tighter. "Rosa, my love. I thought I'd lost you. I'm sorry it took me so long to find you."

Rosa felt giddy with relief, delight, joy—they all combined to steal her voice as her fingers traced Padraic's face. She ignored her pain as she curled into her lover's chest, her face pressed against the steady beating of his heart.

Life is hope.

Damned old woman, why did she always have to be right?

"You're safe now," Padraic said. "I'm getting you out of this godforsaken country."

Rosa shook her head. "No," she said, her voice sounding strange to her. It was raspy, broken from hours of screaming. "We have to go back. We have to go to Paris."

"You're feverish. You don't know what you're saying."

"Listen to me, Padraic," she urged. "I must go back."

He pulled her so tightly to his chest that she lost her breath for a moment as bruises came alive with pain. He quickly released her. "Sorry. Let me get you inside. There's food, medicine. We'll get you healed up, then you'll make more sense."

Rosa let him gather her into his arms and carry her down a path into the woods to a small hunting cabin. She knew as soon as she had her strength back, she'd be returning to Paris, once a city of light and dreams, now the belly of the beast.

She could not abandon her final mission, leave her precious treasure behind.

Chapter 32

Drake had never felt so off balance. He moved in a surreal world of bright lights and loud men, escorting his mother to the medic's rig to be checked out.

Muriel clung to him, but insisted she was unharmed. According to her, other than to duct tape her wrists and mouth, no one had touched her. They'd spent the day driving around, Muriel face-down, a bag over her head, on the floor of the back seat. The driver had been a middle-aged woman with a description that matched that of Natasha Mulo, the missing landlady. She'd been accompanied by a man in his late teens.

Several times they'd pulled to the side of the road and she'd heard the woman outside the car screaming, but then she'd get back inside and drive off as if nothing was wrong.

Other than that, Muriel knew nothing.

The cop in Drake was frustrated by the lack of actionable details. The son in him was ecstatic beyond words to have his mother back safe and sound. And the man who'd had to choose between his mother and the woman he loved was torn apart, a murder of crows pecking at the entrails of his shredded emotions.

Finally, Drake was able to take Muriel back to his apartment so she could rest from her ordeal while he and Jimmy continued to search for Hart. She protested but also understood that he needed her safe before he could go back out, so she finally settled down in the guest bedroom.

While Jimmy coordinated Muriel's protective detail, Drake couldn't resist stealing a few moments of peace before returning to the interminable waiting, all control surrendered to a madman who played with lives like pieces on a chess board.

As he wandered the apartment, the void Hart's absence created was palpable, a wound he could not ignore.

He ended up in his studio, wishing he had time to sit and sketch. There were so many images of Hart in his mind, he wanted to commit them all to some form of permanence so there was no chance they could ever be lost.

No chance he could forget. As if.

Hart's face and body greeted him from every corner of the studio, nowhere more vibrantly than the canvases that held the early studies of *Steadfast*. He couldn't pull his gaze away. That tilt of her jaw, set in stone, immutable, stubborn. The ripple of muscles up her arm and into those shoulders hunched with responsibility and strength. And finally, those eyes—fathomless dark pools that cried out their defiance at the darkness trying to blind them.

Drake's fingers reached out, stroking the painted flesh as if it were real. Then he pulled his hand back. He couldn't give up. She would be back; she had to return. His hand trembled. He clenched it into a fist, his eyes still riveted by Hart's image, as if he could borrow some of her strength and courage.

Tears clouded his vision and he slumped against the table. The remnants of Hart's dress from the unveiling last night brushed against his hand. He clenched it as if reaching for a lifeline and brought it to his face, yearning to find some essence of her, needing to know she was there with him if only in spirit and imagination.

He breathed deep of the soft velvet, inhaling her scent of April showers and springtime blossoms; the smell of rose-tinted sunrises spilling through the window to silhouette her body above his as they made love; the perfume of sweat and exhaled curses as they sparred together, preparing her for her Kempo black belt exam; the laughter he could so seldom coax from her but that was infectious when he could, lightening any task; the crimson of anger when her will and his collided, creating sparks of passion; the silky caress of her hair against his lips.

Drake bowed his head low and let free his tears, his

face buried deep in the folds of a ruined dress. He wept without sound, tears hot and furious, burning his face and throat, choking and gagging him until he was empty of everything but the memory of her face.

She was alive. Somehow he knew the words were true—if only because Kasanov hadn't called to torment him with news of her death.

Hart was alive. And no way in hell was he giving up on her.

He shoved the remnants of the dress aside. Headed out the door, nodding to the uniformed officer who would keep watch over Muriel, he ran down the stairs to where Jimmy waited at the car. Drake tossed him the car keys. "You drive. I need time to think."

"Where to?" Jimmy asked.

"Anton's landlady. Did they find her yet?"

"Taylor said even the FBI couldn't find any trace of her. House isn't in her name. It's in the name of an LLC."

"Let's go pay Taylor a visit—see if we can help the FBI piece this all together."

"Federal building it is." Jimmy put the car in gear and sped away.

Drake got on the phone with Taylor. "Find out what other properties that LLC owns." He closed his eyes for a moment. There was something else... "Oh, and call the ME, ask them about Anton Lavelle's autopsy. Any chance he was already dead when Alicia hit him? Or maybe he was drugged, left there to be run over?"

If his hunch was right, he might have something to trade Kasanov after all. And win Hart's life in return.

Chapter 33

After her surrender, the boys escorted Cassie back inside the service bay, the children following as if she were the Pied Piper. The younger kids cheered and clapped when the older boys forced Cassie back into the Ford's trunk and slammed the lid on her.

They left her there a long time, over an hour by her estimate. Since she was unrestrained, she could move and protect her body, unlike before. This time she suffered no panic attacks. There was nothing to panic about. She had gained Muriel's freedom, which was all that mattered.

Finally, the trunk opened once more. Cassie blinked at the bright lights. Two boys hauled her out. A third, his face bruised and bloody, the guard she had overcome and locked into the bathroom earlier, watched, a submachine gun in his arms and an angry scowl on his face.

This time, they dragged Cassie into what used to be the car dealership's show room area. Kasanov waited, sitting in another expensive leather chair on top a circular dais used to showcase cars. His people sat on the floor on either side of him. Boys nearest him, then girls, and finally young children. There was now another adult, the middle-aged woman she'd seen last night on the steps of the museum. No sign of Vincent; that had to be good. At least she hoped so.

Her captors forced her onto the dais and then down to the floor. They didn't bother with restraints but the four of them arranged themselves behind her, leaving her no path to escape. Fine by her. Her feet were too sore to run anywhere. And where would she run that the dogs wouldn't catch her?

Easier to sit and wait for Drake. He'd be here soon; she was certain.

Everyone was silent for a long moment, Kasanov's people glaring at Cassie as if she were responsible for everything wrong in the world. But not Kasanov. He appeared amused—and angry. A dangerous combination in a man like him.

His expression reminded Cassie of the one her ex-husband used to get when he was drunk and baiting her, setting little traps so that anything she said or did would be the wrong answer and it would be her fault when he lashed out at her.

When she left him, Cassie had vowed never to play those games again. Yet, here she was. But who was playing who?

She opened her mouth to spin another tale, but Kasanov silenced her with a raised hand. "Before you tell me more lies, let me tell you what I know to be true."

The crowd around him leaned forward, as anxious as Cassie to hear what he had to say. All she had to do was keep him talking—or placated enough to listen to her—until the police arrived. To do that, she could use details from his own story and embellish them, twist them to sound like they'd come from the tales Paddy told her.

"My father was Bernard Lavelle of the Lowara," Kasanov began, his voice echoing through the large, glass-walled room. "My mother, Mandra Kasanov, also Lowara. I never knew my father. He died before I was born. Assassinated by a traitor to the Roma."

His eyes grew fierce and he raised a finger to point at Cassie. "Your grandmother, Rosa Costello, and her gaje lover. They murdered my father so they could steal the gold for themselves. That gold is my birthright."

Cassie sat in silence, the weight of Kasanov's accusations pinning her in place.

"Rosa also betrayed my mother. The Nazis had captured her. That gold was my father's only bargaining chip to gain her freedom. When he failed to deliver it, they shipped my mother to the camps. First Ravensbrück and then Auschwitz-Birkenau."

An audible moan of dismay came from the crowd behind him, several of the girls—led by the woman, Natasha—making shrill noises of grieving, slapping their bodies and faces. Once again Cassie thought about this strange family Natasha and Nickolai had created. More cult than family from what Vincent had told her.

"I was born in Birkenau," Kasanov continued. "Somehow, thanks to my mother, we survived when so many others did not. She raised me to never forget. That no matter where I went or what I did, my heart was Roma. That a blood debt must always be repaid."

He stood, glaring down at Cassie. "And tonight that debt has come due."

Two guards held her in place as the other two left and returned, carrying a khaki vest bristling with wires, pockets bulging with what looked like plastic explosives. Cassie tried to struggle, but it was useless.

"What have you done?" Cassie cried out from where she knelt on the floor, hoping to warn the children. As the first two pinned her down, the other two lowered the vest over her head and secured it with chains and a padlock.

The vest was heavy—at least twenty pounds—and she had no idea how the explosives were triggered, but there was a mercury level sitting at the top of the vest's neckline, forcing her to hold still, barely breathing. "You'll kill us all."

⚬⊙⚬

As Jimmy drove, Drake leaned back in his seat and allowed the city streets to blur around him. He felt exhausted, not just physically, but emotionally and mentally. Ever since Steadfast went up in flames last night—God, was it only last night?—his mind had been speeding through a maze filled with twists, turns, and dead ends.

"A scavenger hunt," he muttered.

"More like smoke and mirrors," Jimmy said. "Sending us in one direction while he moves in another."

"Herding us like cattle." Drake sat upright. "I'm not even sure Alicia actually killed Anton or that this is about his death at all. I can't stop thinking...something Hart used to say about her grandmother..."

"What?" Jimmy scoffed. "Don't tell me we're resorting to gypsy fortune telling now? I know Hart acts like she can really hear her grandmother's ghost, but—"

"Ghost. That's it. The alias the landlady used, Natasha Mulo. Mulo is the gypsy word for ghost."

"So? There's plenty of gypsies in Eastern Europe. No reason why they couldn't be partnered with Kasanov."

"The Roma don't usually partner with outsiders. Gaje, they call us. They stick with their own clans. It's all about family." He thought back to Kasanov's words earlier. "If Anton was Kasanov's grandson, then Natasha is probably related to him as well. What if they're all Roma?"

Jimmy shrugged. "Not sure how that would make a difference. Gangsters are gangsters."

"All those women he killed when he was younger. It's

been bothering me—they all look like Rosa. The way he tortured them, it was like it was personal."

"Or like he's a sadistic psycho nut job."

Drake buried his face in his hands, his fingers raking through his hair as he strained to remember everything Hart had told him about Rosa.

Think, Drake, think. He closed his eyes for a moment. He remembered Hart smoothing his hand over Rosa's quilt, her voice hypnotic, boring its way into his soul as she told the story of how the quilt saved her grandmother's life. A warm tingling flowed through him just as it had that night, from Hart's hand into his heart. But the details—they were vague.

Another memory hit him with jackhammer ferocity. Hart, naked in bed, still flushed with their lovemaking, embarrassed that she'd hurled a Gypsy—no, Roma, she'd called it Roma—curse at him earlier when they'd been arguing. He couldn't even remember now what the fight was about, it had ended like all of their fights—in bed with no one losing, a satisfying resolution for all parties.

Drake shook his head in frustration. He couldn't remember the words, just the images—the delicate flush of Hart's skin as she blushed in embarrassment, the crooked smile she'd given him, the gleam in her eyes as she'd defended her grandmother despite the fact that Rosa's people had cast her out, shunned her.

What else, what else? There was more, he knew it. He just couldn't force the memories to the surface right now, not with everything else clouding his mind. Including that last image of Hart, head turned to look over her naked shoulder, smiling at him, making him feel like he was the only man in creation.

"What if this is really about Hart? And her grandmother?" he asked Jimmy. "Nothing to do with me or my being a cop."

"Then what the hell has Anton's death or Alicia or the fact that you were named in his case file have to do with anything?"

"I was the detective on call that weekend. Maybe the whole thing was a set up?"

"To what end? If Kasanov wanted Hart, he could have taken her at any time. Ditto for you or Alicia. And why kill his own grandson, the one he was depending on to save the family business? It doesn't make sense."

They sped across the Hot Metal Bridge. "You're right. I just feel like we're missing something." He broke off as they pulled into the federal building. A few minutes later, they were back in the situation room with Prescott, Taylor, and Texas.

"Do you have anything?" Drake asked. They all looked up with bleary eyes, each shaking their heads. Even Prescott appeared less than dapper, his suit jacket wrinkled and creased, a coffee stain marring his silk tie.

"Medical examiner wasn't much help," Texas started. "Said Anton was definitely alive when he was run over and his tox screen was negative. But there are a ton of things they don't test for on the routine tox screen that could have incapacitated him. Also, he didn't have the typical pattern of injuries resulting from being thrown up onto the car on impact, so it is possible that he was already down when struck, but there's no way to prove it."

"How about you two?" Prescott asked Drake and Jimmy. "Did you find anything at the warehouse where they left your mother? Has she remembered anything helpful?"

"No, but I might have. Those women Kasanov killed when he was younger, were any of them gypsy? Roma?" Drake asked.

Prescott frowned at him as if he'd begun speaking in tongues, but Taylor jerked his head up from his computer. "How'd you know that? They all were—and so were some other deaths I found attributed to Kasanov. They weren't all women, some were men. Signs of torture as well as signs of someone searching for something at their crime scenes."

Drake exchanged glances with Jimmy. "Rosa Costello Hart—Cassie's grandmother," he began, his voice gaining breakneck speed as he tried to tell them everything he could remember. "She was a Kalderasha gypsy. Hart told me when she was young, in—" he searched his memory, listened for her voice in his memory, "1936, there was a meeting of the gypsy families. They were going to travel together, protect each other, and escape from Hitler. But their camp was attacked. Rosa and a few other women—no one else from her clan," he frowned, that wasn't the word Hart had used, but close enough, "survived. They took Rosa to a work farm but she escaped to," he stumbled, "Budapest. Then she travelled across Europe and eventually joined the French Resistance. She met her husband, Padraic Hart, when she rescued him after his ship was sunk by a U-boat off the French coast."

Texas held up a hand, scribbling furiously. Drake noted that the agent also had a tape recorder going.

Prescott rocked forward with anticipation. "Good, what else? Any mention of Kasanov?"

"None that I heard of. They got married, moved to Pennsylvania after the war and lived happily ever after." He frowned. "Hart told me once that Rosa was shunned, declared unclean, by her people because she married an outsider."

"Did she give you any details? Names? Places? Dates?"

"No—to her it was ancient family history—stories to pass on to her own kids someday…" His voice trailed off as he finished that thought to its logical conclusion.

To Hart's conclusion—dead and buried, no kids. She would have made a wonderful mother. He had to swallow hard before he could face the others.

"Does Hart have anything of her grandmother's?" Prescott persisted, unwilling to drop any investigative thread, no matter how flimsy. "Journals? Photos?"

"No." The single syllable was all Drake could manage.

"Cassie lost everything when her house burned down this summer," Jimmy finished for him.

Prescott looked up at that. "Arson?" he asked, an

eager gleam in his eye.

"Yes, but the actor wasn't Kasanov," Jimmy assured him.

"So we need to find friends of Rosa Costello, people she may have confided in. Somewhere she and Kasanov must have crossed paths. He's looking for something, something important enough to keep him searching for all these years."

"A quest," Drake whispered.

Jimmy nodded eagerly. "Maybe not one of his own choosing either. Maybe something passed down generations, even."

"Like a blood feud? Until it found the twisted, sick sonofabitch willing to see it through to the bitter end."

Prescott was nodding in unison with them. "God help us, it makes sense in a warped sort of way."

"How does this help us find him now? And Hart?" Drake asked, feeling more frustrated than ever.

"Maybe it doesn't, but this might," Taylor said. "Here's a list of properties held by the same LLC as the house Anton Lavelle lived in." Several photos and satellite imagery popped up on the screen. All businesses that would make it easy to launder cash the old-fashioned way, without computer manipulation: a dry cleaner, convenience store, used car dealership turned salvage yard, and a fast food restaurant.

"There. Where's that one at?" Drake said, pointing to the salvage operation. It was perfect. Secluded, off the main highway, fenced in with security that wouldn't draw any undue attention. Perfect location to hide vehicles—or a hostage.

"Off Noblestown Road, southwest of Carnegie," Taylor answered.

"Out of our jurisdiction," Jimmy said.

"But not ours," Prescott put in. "Taylor, start working on warrants. Call the locals, arrange for a drive by of each of these properties."

"Call the sheriff's department," Drake added. "They have FLIR on their helicopter, can use the infrared to see if anyone is inside any of those buildings. It will be faster and safer than sending patrol cars." He headed toward the door. No more sitting and watching while others did the work of saving Hart.

"Wait," Prescott called after him. "Hart could be at any one of them. If we can't pinpoint which one, then the only way to make sure they don't know we're coming is to arrange to hit them simultaneously."

Drake ignored him. Done with waiting, he was already out the door, Jimmy hard on his heels.

Chapter 34

AS DRAKE DROVE to the old car dealership, Jimmy called for backup from the sheriff's department and filled them in. He never questioned Drake's actions—that was the great thing about Jimmy, he trusted Drake's gut almost as much as Drake himself did.

"They're twenty minutes out on the copter," he said as he hung up.

"We're closer than that." Drake twisted the wheel and headed down an unmarked side street that, in typical Carnegie fashion, seemed to lead right off the edge of a ravine before making an abrupt turn. Streets around here would go from two lanes to a single lane to gravel and back to cobblestone or pavement without warning. It was a maze that few ventured, but the fastest way to get to Noblestown

Road from the federal building. Much faster than the main highways the patrol cars would be following.

They'd just turned on to Noblestown when Drake's phone rang. Jimmy answered for him. "It's dispatch. They say some kid called in, told them Hart's at the scrapyard."

"I knew it. Where is this kid? We need to know what we're walking in on."

"Slow down—he's waiting for us at that Sheetz up ahead."

Drake hit the brakes while Jimmy listened some more then hung up. "The sheriff's department is mobilizing."

"Mobilizing who? SWAT?" Last thing he needed was for a bunch of cowboys to rush in and get Hart killed.

Jimmy glanced at him, lips pressed together. "And the bomb squad."

THE KID WAS maybe twelve, scrawny, dark-haired, wearing filthy jeans, and a windbreaker two sizes too large. He sat in a booth of the brightly lit convenience store devouring his second chili-cheese dog with all the trimmings while Drake went over a sketch of the scrapyard's layout with him.

"So you saw them bury bombs here, here, and here?"

The kid, Vincent was his name, nodded, chili juice running down his chin. He ate like he hadn't had a decent meal in months.

"And there are motion detectors here and here?"

"They're probably wired as well," Jimmy said. "Guy's got the whole damn place covered. There's no way to get an assault team in there. And with the wrecks all around it, no sight lines for a sniper."

Vincent gulped and swallowed. "Cassie climbed the magnet—it's on a crane. Goes real high. Would that help?"

"If we can get past the guards—you said there were four? We have to assume they all carry detonators as well as guns." Jimmy scowled at the map as only a former marine could. He shook his head. "Maybe rope down from the copter?"

"What if he has the roof rigged as well?" Drake argued. "That's what I would do." He thought about it. "It's a one-man job. Go in, take out the guards—"

"With what? If they have dead man switches—"

A SUV screeched into the parking lot and came to a stop. Drake glanced out the window. Sheriff's department. A woman wearing a tactical uniform hopped out and strode into the store. He smiled as he recognized her: Amanda Devlin, the lead bomb squad technician.

"Mandy, just the person we need."

"My guys are on the way with the disposal unit, but I live nearby, so came ahead. What's up?"

Drake filled her in. "A full assault is out—we don't know what kind of manual trigger the bombs have. But I think I can get in there if we have some way to take out the possibility of remote detonation."

She raised an eyebrow at that. "Not your jurisdiction,

so forget that. But come with me. I've got your remote detonation problem solved."

They left the boy in the care of the clerk and went out to her SUV. She opened the rear. "Meet ACE, boys. Our Alleghany County Emergency UAV. Equipped with radio and cell jamming capabilities as well as thermal and infrared cameras and omnidirectional microphones."

"What are we waiting for?" Drake said.

"You are waiting for me to get the rest of my team, brief them, and take care of bringing the hostages out safely. Go back inside and grab some coffee while I update my guys and the SWAT boys. Don't worry. This will all be over before you know it."

Drake glared at her. She was right. It wasn't his jurisdiction, wasn't protocol to go in before the team was deployed. The protocol existed to prevent loss of life.

It also wasn't the woman she loved trapped inside there with a madman, surrounded by bombs—at least five that the kid knew about, who knew how many more?

He spun on his heel and strode past Mandy to his car, Jimmy on his heels.

"Drake," she shouted. "Damn it! Don't you—"

Her words were cut out as he slammed the car door and started the engine. Jimmy hopped in the other side and they sped out of the parking lot. "Hope you know what you're doing," Jimmy said. "Remember, it's not just Hart in there. Vincent said there were kids as well."

"There's a way in, but it's a one man job," Drake

argued as they raced down the road. Lights appeared behind them, but Mandy's Tahoe was no match for Drake's Mustang.

"If Vincent's intel is accurate. He's just a kid, wouldn't have access to all of their perimeter defenses."

"I can handle the guys on the ground. You just make sure Mandy gets that drone deployed."

Drake spotted the turn off for the scrapyard. He cut his lights and slowed down as the Mustang bounced onto the dirt road. He pulled off the road and into a clearing—if he did his job right, there would be plenty of other vehicles needing to use this road later tonight.

He popped the trunk and grabbed his ballistic vest along with the Remington 700 pump action shotgun he stored there.

"Once Mandy jams the radio and cell phones, we won't be able to talk," Jimmy reminded him.

"I thought of that," Drake said, grabbing one last thing from the trunk. A can of fluorescent spray paint.

Mandy's SUV, its lights out, pulled in behind them.

"That's my cue." Drake ran into the trees, heading for the break in the fence Vincent had told them about. Behind him, he heard Mandy and Jimmy arguing, but their voices were low and soon faded into the night.

Now it was up to him.

CHAPTER 35

THE BOYS FINISHED securing the bomb vest to Cassie, retrieved their guns, and stood back. Kasanov left his chair and moved to look each one in the eye, nodding at them as if he were a general inspecting his troops. "Well done. Don't forget to kennel the dogs before you activate the motion detectors. You know what needs to be done."

The boys moved behind Cassie and out of sight. Kasanov turned his attention to the other children who sat on the floor behind the dais. While he'd addressed the guards, the older woman, Natasha, had brought out a pitcher and began serving drinks to the children. They ranged in age from eight or nine to their teens. As they accepted their paper cups of what looked like orange juice, Kasanov moved behind them, stroking their hair, kissing them on the head, and whispering something to each as they drank. It seemed like some kind of bizarre bedtime ritual.

With the showroom spotlights aimed down on him, glinting from his gray hair like a halo, the whole affair took on a surreal quality. As if he'd hypnotized the children. They beamed up at him and drank, each placing an empty cup on the floor in front of them.

At first Cassie didn't realize what she was witnessing. When she did, it was with a sick feeling that roiled through her stomach. "Stop," she shouted, keeping the rest of her body frozen in place. "Don't drink that."

Kasanov caught her eye and shook his head in disapproval. He'd come to the end of the row of children, the last, the youngest, sitting in his lap as she finished her cup of juice. He gently moved her to the floor and returned to his seat.

He pulled out a small remote, the kind that could start a car. "It's active now, Dr. Hart. Any movement and it will explode, taking all of us. But if you do nothing, they will all die anyway. How frustrating it must be for you. The doctor who never gives up on her patients, who chases after any lost cause no matter the danger to herself, and here you are, forced to sit and watch these innocent children die."

"This has nothing to do with Rosa or any treasure," Cassie said, trying to reason with Kasanov. Drake would be here soon, was all she could think. "Why are you doing this? And to your own family?"

Kasanov stretched his legs out and crossed them at the ankle as if he didn't have a care in the world. "First of all, they aren't my family. Merely random strays Natasha collected and taught some basic street skills to. Useful, but disposable."

Cassie glanced past him to see if the children responded to his declaration, but they all had their eyes half-closed, slouching or lying across the floor in a stupor. Whatever he'd given them, it acted too quickly to be cyanide, the poison of choice among cult leaders like Jim Jones. Maybe a benzodiazepam or barbituate?

"Second," Kasanov continued, "this has everything to do with your grandmother and her treasure. Do you know how she killed my father?"

His voice grew shrill, despite his relaxed posture. Unsure of how to respond and not wanting to agitate him further, Cassie merely shook her head.

"She knew that treasure was my father's only chance to save his wife and unborn child. But Rosa didn't care. She tricked him; let him and the Nazis he was working with follow her deep into the catacombs below Paris. They thought she was leading them to the gold, but instead she led them into a trap. They reached a dead end and she blew up the cavern, thousands of tons of rock came down on top of them."

He leaned forward, both elbows on his knees, his voice dropping as if he whispered a prayer. "Imagine how they died. Crushed under the weight, broken and bloody, slowly suffocating as the air went out, or drowning in their own blood. I want you to picture that, Dr. Hart. Because that's exactly how you will die here, tonight."

Kneeling and holding her position for so long beneath the weight of the bomb had her entire body aching, ready to collapse. She just had to stay strong long enough for Drake to get here.

Then Kasanov surprised her. He leaned back and said, "I really thought Drake would have figured it out sooner."

Cassie frowned at that, trying hard not to move. "You want him to come here?"

"Of course. I want him to suffer as I have. Knowing that you were the cause of all this death and destruction. They can see us clearly through the showroom window— it's why I chose this place. They'll call for SWAT and the bomb squad, whoever. Drake will be forced to watch. I'll wait until the first wave of officers comes in, trips the motion detectors. Or if their SWAT team snipers kill me, then this," he raised his fist with the detonator, "will set the bomb off as soon as my grip loosens."

"A dead man's switch."

"Exactly." He beamed at her as if she were a slow student who had finally gotten an answer correct. "I didn't come here tonight to learn about a treasure. I came here tonight to die. With you, Dr. Hart."

Chapter 36

• ‖ ⁑•▷◐◁•⁑ ‖ •

THE HOLE VINCENT had used to escape the fenced in scrapyard was hardly a hole, Drake discovered. More like a place where the dogs had dug out a few inches of dirt below the fence. Still, the dirt was loose and it was easy enough to enlarge it to accommodate the larger bulk of a full-grown man wearing a tactical vest. He just hated wasting the time.

He knelt in the dirt and used the stock of the shotgun to dig, jabbing it furiously into the earth and ramming the soil out of his way. Usually, situations like this, he was able to keep his heart rate low, slow his breathing, stay focused and in control. But after everything that had happened in the past twenty-four hours, knowing Hart was in there along with innocent children, knowing the killing spree

Kasanov had gleefully left in his wake, there was no way in hell Drake was in control. What he felt was the exact opposite of being in command of the situation, more like a berserker frenzy.

Which was exactly why Mandy Devlin hadn't wanted him involved. Too much emotion, too much adrenaline, and he could get everyone killed.

He cleared enough space beneath the fence. Shedding his vest, he stacked it and the shotgun against the fence and belly crawled through. Spitting dirt, he reached back and dragged the Remington and his vest through, then knelt there for a moment, his vision hazed red. *Breathe, damn it.* His fingers fumbled the vest back into place, a quick check of the pockets to make sure he still had the flex-cuffs, extra ammo, paint can, OC spray, and flashlight.

Still shaky and breathing too fast, he climbed to his feet. Saw a shadow overhead: the drone. He waved at it and it did a quick circle in acknowledgment. Mandy had come through with the cell and radio jammer. He drew in a deep breath. Finally, something had gone right tonight.

Time to finish this.

His plan was simple: take out the guards and sneak into the car dealership while the SWAT team got in position. Vincent had shown him how to access the car building via a side entrance away from the bombs—Kasanov's exit strategy, Drake guessed.

He skirted the piles of broken-down vehicles until the blazing lights of the car dealership came into sight. The large, plate-glass windows of the showroom revealed everything: children lying still on the floor, Kasanov standing, holding a detonator in one hand and a pistol in the other, and Hart. Kneeling. With a suicide bomb vest strapped to her body.

Time for a change of plan.

❦

"YOU DID ALL this, killed innocent people, just to kill yourself?" Cassie asked.

"They weren't all innocent. Certainly not Alicia Fairstone. In a way, you owe your fate to her. She killed my grandson, Anton. Anton was to be the future of my little enterprise. He would carry on my bloodline. Without him, I'm nothing. There's nothing left for me. Except death. A death of my choosing, not some random whim of fate."

Cassie looked past him to the children who all now lay unconscious on the floor. "That's ridiculous. Look at those children. You could have raised one of them to carry on—"

He leapt to his feet. "Blood is everything," he thundered down at her. "My worthless daughter, Natasha, might be content leaving my legacy to *gaje*, but that's not why my father died, not what my mother taught me."

Speaking of Natasha, where was she? The woman had vanished. Cassie focused on the immediate problem—reasoning with Kasanov. "Please. They're just children."

281

"You think I care? That I haven't killed women and children before? I had a lot of fun in my youth searching out women who could have been Rosa—I even killed my fellow Roma and others who knew her during the war, trying to find her. You see, she disappeared so completely we could find no trace. My mother didn't know Padraic Hart's name, much less where they might have taken the gold. It wasn't until the Berlin wall came down and the Stasi opened its archives that I even found a photo of Rosa."

"That was almost fifty years after she left France—you were still looking for her?"

"Of course. She owed me a blood debt. I was not about to forget that. By then I had lost much of the fury that drove me as a youth, learned more patience. With the info I found in the Stasi files, I tracked her here, to Pennsylvania, but then lost her once more. When it came time to get Anton the computer skills necessary to revitalize our family enterprise, I sent him here with Natasha and she kept looking."

His face twisted with pain. "Fate is cruel, though. After Anton was killed, when I saw the police file and investigated the detectives involved in his case, I found Drake—and photos of you, the spitting image of Rosa. Too late to save my family, but never too late to savor vengeance."

"Do it, then," she challenged him. It was the only way she could save Drake and the other police officers. He'd be here soon. "Kill me now. Let's die together."

His grimace of pain turned triumphant. "It won't be that easy. Not for the last person on earth who has Rosa Costello's blood. You deserve a fate that will make the universe forever curse her name as I have. And your Drake? He'll be a withered husk of a man after tonight, after he witnesses what you have caused. Guilt will gnaw at him, eat him alive, twist and tear at his heart better than any torture I could devise. You'll die knowing you destroyed the man you love. It's not the justice my father deserves, but it's the closest thing I can give him."

Tears burned Cassie's eyes even though she didn't dare wipe them away for fear of detonating the bomb. She should, she knew. Just jump up, end it all before Drake or the other police officers came in and got themselves killed.

But she couldn't. Not because she was afraid of dying, rather because she could not give up hope. Life is hope.

Typical Rosa. Always had to be right.

Drake would find a way. He always did.

CHAPTER 37

THE DOGS BEGAN barking. Kasanov stopped his frenetic pacing and smiled down at Cassie. "Sounds like Drake has finally arrived. Better late than never." He straightened his shoulders and raised his gun to aim it at Cassie's head. "Let's see if the SWAT snipers are paying attention."

Nothing happened. No laser sights aimed at Kasanov, no shot shattering the windows. He frowned.

"You didn't think it would be that easy, did you?" came a man's voice from a hallway on the far side of the showroom.

Cassie's hope died. It was Drake. Accompanied by two of Kasanov's guards. They shoved him forward and beamed triumphantly.

Drake winked at Cassie, then focused his attention on Kasanov. She wanted to run to him, leap into his arms. She wanted to slap him silly for walking into Kasanov's trap— what the hell was he thinking?

Most of all, she wanted him gone. Far from here. Safe.

Pinned in place by the bomb, she could have none of that.

Kasanov appeared equally unhappy. He whirled on the two guards, raised his pistol and shot them both in the face before they could respond. Their bodies slumped to the floor. Drake froze, hands raised in surrender.

"You were supposed to be watching," Kasanov shouted at Drake. "Where the hell is your bloody SWAT team? Why haven't they ended this?"

"I haven't given them the signal to," Drake said calmly. As if he were in charge.

"Then you can go to hell." Kasanov raised his hand with the detonator.

Cassie kept her eyes open. Drake was still a good ten feet away, too far for her to touch, but if she was going to die, she wanted him to be the last thing she saw. He smiled at her. Not a sad smile, not a "good-bye forever, I love you" smile.

More like a, "don't worry, we can handle this" smile.

Kasanov pressed the button. Nothing happened.

Before Drake could make a move, Kasanov swung on Cassie. He lowered his pistol, resting it against her forehead. "There's a mercury switch on her bomb," he told Drake. "I so much as bump her and it blows."

Drake nodded as if he'd expected this. "I came here to update you on Alicia Fairstone. Turns out we won't be charging her with murder after all."

"What are you talking about?" Kasanov's voice was tight with fury.

"She's innocent. Your grandson was already lying dead on that road before her car hit him."

"But how—who?" The gun pressed against Cassie's forehead bounced with energy. It took everything she had to not let it rock her body.

"I think maybe it was his landlady," Drake said in a calm voice as if they were playing a game and he'd just suggested the killer was Colonel Mustard in the library with the lead pipe. "Not exactly sure why. But when we went back and interviewed his friends at school, we learned he was saving money, planning to move out. And he'd already approached his professors about job opportunities with several *Fortune 500* companies."

"No. He'd never..." Kasanov shook his head. "Young, foolish, traitor."

"Natasha had to punish him." Cassie tried to fill in the blanks, help Drake. She had a feeling he was bluffing. Despite the fact his face was devoid of emotion, she was expert in reading his body language. He wasn't as confident as he sounded. "Natasha could never let him betray you like that—she was loyal to you, to your family."

Kasanov frowned in thought. He glanced around, seemed to realize Natasha had vanished.

Drake picked up on it as well. "Or maybe the opposite. Maybe she liked living here as well, feared that if Anton left her, pursued his own dreams, then she'd be abandoned, left behind to face you and take the blame. I imagine she knows better than anyone how you reward failure."

"I'll kill the bitch—" Kasanov faltered, obviously seeing the paradox. He'd boxed himself in.

"Lower the weapon and surrender," Drake coaxed him. Cassie realized that as they talked, he'd been edging forward, getting into position to tackle Kasanov. But he'd have to do it without knocking into her or allowing Kasanov to move her.

Kasanov appeared to actually consider it. He straightened, his gun leaving Cassie's forehead—although still aimed at her.

The glass behind her cracked. A dark spot appeared directly between Kasanov's eyebrows. Drake hurtled through the air to push Kasanov's body away from Cassie.

They crashed to the floor. Kasanov's foot knocked into Cassie's arm. She held her breath, tightened every muscle in her body, and strained to hold still, her gaze fixated on the silver mercury in its glass enclosure. It jiggled and slid a hair's breadth to one side.

And then Drake was there. Kneeling in front of her, steadying her. The mercury stabilized. Cassie looked up, let her breath out.

"Sorry I'm late to the party," he said. He rested his forehead against hers, his hands bracing her shoulders, keeping her still and safe.

CHAPTER 38

"Muriel?" Cassie whispered. "Is she okay?"

"She's fine. They never hurt her—had some woman scream as if she was being tortured, but all they did was drive her around in circles."

"You need to leave. Take the children with you," Cassie begged. "Please, Drake. Think of your mother. And those kids need you. Start with the smallest, they'll need treatment faster than the others."

Footsteps sounded from the same direction Drake had come from. A woman carrying a toolbox and wheeling what looked like a tiny cement mixer joined them.

"I'm Mandy Devlin. I'll be your friendly neighborhood bomb removal expert today. Now let's see what we have here." She put her hand on Drake's shoulder. "You need to step back now, Drake."

He nodded and moved reluctantly to one side, ending up at the body of one of the guards. He bent and retrieved his service weapon, holstering it, then stepped as close to Cassie as he could without getting in Mandy's way. Too close. Cassie felt her strength ebb, knew she couldn't hold out much longer.

"No," Cassie said to both Mandy and Drake. "Get the children out first. He poisoned them, I don't know with what, but they need to get to a hospital."

"Sorry," Mandy answered. "I can't let anyone else in here until we defuse this. Can't risk it."

"Drake, you have to do it, then."

Mandy concentrated on a dental mirror she used to examine every nook and cranny of the bomb vest. "She's right. Go. Now. Just make sure you follow the same path out as you did coming in. We can't completely clear the building of the other IEDs until I finish here."

Drake crouched down, one palm on each side of Cassie's face. "I'll be back."

He left Cassie and ran to grab the two smallest of the children, one slung over his shoulder, the other in his arms, and left. Mandy took his place in front of Cassie, her toolbox open beside her.

"How come you're not wearing one of those bomb suits?" Cassie asked, not sure if that was a good thing or not.

"You ever try one of those on? They take forever to get

into, weigh like ninety pounds, and smell like a football team's unwashed jockstraps. Ugh. Trust me, something like this, we're both better with me going hands-on—not like the suit would actually save me from this kind of blast."

"Why didn't it go off when you killed Kasanov?"

"We jammed the radio and cell transmissions. Thanks to Drake giving us a head's up so we had time to get here and have our equipment ready to go. I don't think your friend," she jerked her chin at Kasanov, "was anticipating us getting here so fast."

"No. He was expecting you to storm in—" Cassie remembered something Kasanov had said. "Did you deactivate the motion detectors? He said they'd trigger the bomb. He also said there were more."

"That's why I'm the only one here. But yes, we got the motion detectors. We'll clear the rest of the building—" She was interrupted by Drake's return. "Thought we got rid of you."

"Told you, I'd be back. I'll get the kids out—no need to risk anyone else. You just get her free of that goddamn bomb." He grunted as he hoisted another kid, this one bigger, across his shoulder, and then squatted to lift a little girl into his arms.

Mandy withdrew a small aerosol canister along with some wire from her toolkit. "Here's how this will work. First, I'll set up a bypass circuit. Then I'll freeze the mercury switch and cut it loose so you can move. Finally, I'll disarm the secondary trigger and cut the vest off you. Easy-peasy, one-two-three."

Cassie nodded. Her legs had gone numb beneath the weight of her body kneeling in the same position for so long and her arms were trembling from the pressure of holding her upright. "Just hurry."

She couldn't see what Mandy was doing, but the bomb technician hummed a merry tune—Drowning Pool's, "Bodies," the same song Cassie used to teach CPR to first responders—as she clipped and snipped wires near the mercury switch. Then she used the aerosol spray. Freezing cold droplets hit Cassie's breastbone.

"Sorry about that," Mandy murmured. She finished spraying and moved in with wire clippers. "Okay, that's done, you can move a little."

"I'm kinda stuck. Are you finished?"

"Hold on, just one more second." She moved around to Cassie's back and began to work there. Drake returned, smiled at Cassie, and gave her a thumb's up as he gathered a teenaged girl into his arms.

"Hey, lover boy," Mandy called to him. "Tell my guys they can come in and remove the other casualties—only them, you show them the route. Got it?"

"Got it."

The sound of wires being cut came as Mandy's hands moved over the blocks of explosives. "Most people don't realize it, but trigger devices—in this case, blasting caps— can cause a heck of an explosion on their own. And we don't want that, do we?"

"No, ma'am." It was nice to be able to breathe and shift her weigh—although the movement released a barrage of stabbing pain up her legs.

Mandy kept working. Drake returned, accompanied by three more men—enough to remove the rest of the kids. He came and sat in front of Cassie, letting her lean her weight onto him, her arms over his shoulders, their foreheads bowed together. "You know, after this, my wedding surprise for you is going to seem really, really lame."

She couldn't stop the laughter that shook through her.

"Can we save the jokes for later?" Mandy asked. "Just a few more to go."

Cassie and Drake sat obediently silent, simply staring into each other's eyes. Somehow, with him there, Cassie wasn't afraid of anything. Mandy deposited the blasting caps into the same special container she'd placed the mercury switch into then pulled a pair of trauma shears from her toolkit. "Ready to cut this sucker off? As a fashion accessory, it kinda clashes with your dress."

Before Cassie could say anything, Mandy sliced the vest down the back. Drake stood and steadied Cassie's arms as Mandy slid the vest, the chains, and padlock, now dangling useless, over her head.

And she was free.

Mandy carefully packed the vest into her bombproof container and rolled it out. "Follow me out," she ordered. "Drake, you know the way. We still need to get the dog in and clear the building of any other IEDs."

"We'll be right behind you," Drake said.

Cassie tried to move but her legs rebelled. "I can't stand." Her words came out as a stutter while chills shook her entire body. Drake took his windbreaker off and helped her into it.

"I've got you," he said as he raised her in his arms, cradling her against his chest. She threw one arm around the back of his neck and hung on. "I seem to recall having to carry you like this when we met at our first crime scene." He carefully followed Mandy's route past the offices toward the side door. "Is it going to be a habit?"

"I vote for no," she answered, too exhausted to come up with anything clever.

As he turned down the short corridor leading to the exit, she glimpsed movement from the corner of her eye. Natasha rushed forward, holding a dagger, eyes wide with fury.

"Drake," Cassie called out a warning.

He spun around. But of course he couldn't reach his gun—he had his hands full with Cassie. She stretched her hand down to where his gun was holstered over his kidney and slid it free. Natasha screamed incoherently as she lunged toward them.

Cassie brought the gun up over Drake's shoulder and fired it just as he'd taught her, aiming for the center mass and not stopping until the threat was taken care of.

The booming sounds of the shots fired in the cramped

space were deafening. Natasha staggered forward despite the first shots hitting her chest, then finally fell to the ground. Cassie realized she wasn't the only one shooting; Mandy was taking aim from beyond them in the doorway.

Drake rushed Cassie outside as Mandy and her teammates moved in to check on Natasha. Jimmy met them at a junked-up Impala that was missing its doors but still had its rear seat. He helped Drake lower Cassie onto the seat.

"You two okay?" he asked as he pried Drake's gun from Cassie's hand.

His words reverberated through Cassie's brain, mixing with the pound of the gunshots. She frowned at Drake. "You didn't drop me to go for your gun."

He grinned down at her. "Of course not. There was no time. I knew you could handle it."

"Have to say," Jimmy said, "that was some pretty good teamwork in there."

Cassie glanced at the gun in his hand. They wouldn't know until the autopsy if she'd killed Natasha or if Mandy did. She wasn't sure if it mattered. "How are the kids?"

Jimmy answered. "Paramedics said it looks like some kind of sedative. They're using a reversal agent. Said they should be okay. We got to them just in time."

As if hearing that relieved him of the burden of remaining professional, Drake sank down to crouch in front of her, tears in his eyes. If she had the strength left, she'd be crying as well. She took his hands in both of hers; they were trembling. The aftermath of adrenaline... and more.

She tried to lighten the mood. "See what happens when you insist on a wedding? Your mom is going to kill me when she sees this dress."

CHAPTER 39

THEY'D JUST GOTTEN back home from hours of debriefing and barely had a chance to shower and greet Muriel when Adeena called. "You need to get over here. Tessa's having a fit, says she has to talk to you and Drake. Now."

Drake had resisted, but Cassie knew the trauma of having your home turned into a violent crime scene. "It's the least we can do."

And so, with the dawn light shimmering down, they drove to Tessa's house. On the way there, Drake got a call from Jimmy, who was at the hospital with the children. It was a quick conversation, mainly him listening as Cassie waited impatiently. Finally, he hung up.

"Are the kids okay?" she asked.

"Docs say they'll all be fine. A few are talking—filling

in the blanks. Sounds like Kasanov and his daughter had a love-hate relationship. She adored him, would do anything for him, and he treated her like dirt. To him, the only thing Natasha ever did right was to have a son to carry on the family bloodline."

"Not too surprising."

"Anyway, apparently Anton enjoyed being a college student a little too much. Got into drugs—mainly Ecstasy and other MDMA variants, a little heroin as well."

"Ecstasy wouldn't show up in a routine tox screen," she put in. "And if he hadn't used heroin in a while, it might not either."

"Right. Which explains why the ME didn't pick up on the fact that he'd OD'd. Natasha panicked, thought he was dead. But she'd already been searching for her father's other obsession—"

"Rosa and the treasure." Cassie could fill in the blanks. "She must have already known about you and me, so she dumped Anton in an area where she knew you'd be called to investigate, thinking that would cover her tracks and keep Kasanov from suspecting what really happened."

"Irony is Anton wasn't even dead. He was still alive when Alicia hit him."

"She killed her own son." Cassie shook her head. "All of this because of a crazy blood feud from over half a century ago. I just don't understand some people."

"I think maybe that's not such a bad thing," Drake assured her.

They pulled up in front of Tessa's house. Adeena opened the door and led them to the living room. The presents from yesterday were now piled on the floor around the coffee table. Tessa sat in the middle of the couch, an old, hand-carved wooden box cradled in her lap.

"I told you," she said, her voice strident. "I need to give you your wedding present."

"Tessa," Cassie said as gently as possible, "can we maybe do this tomorrow?" She didn't add that right now they had a wedding to cancel.

"Why?" the old woman demanded. "You're getting married tonight and Rosa told me to give this to you on the day you married your soul mate. That's today."

Drake sat down beside Tessa and took her hand in his. He met Cassie's eyes. "I'm sure Rosa couldn't have envisioned that our wedding would be disrupted by a madman."

"Of course she did. Rosa had the Sight. Not as powerful as her own grandmother, but strong enough to know what was coming. Just as she knew that Cassandra's first husband was not her true soul mate." Tessa slapped her hand down on the small cedar box, hard enough to rattle it. "Open it. Learn the truth of Rosa's gold."

Drake shrugged one shoulder. Cassie looked to him and Adeena, who said, "You know Tessa. Might as well do what she says or you'll be here all day arguing."

Cassie sank down to sit on the floor, leaning against Drake's legs, and pulled the box onto her lap. It wasn't very heavy, obviously hand-made. She traced her fingers over the carvings that covered it.

"Padraic made it," Tessa said. "Go on. Open it. See what Rosa and Padraic kept secret all these years."

With trembling fingers, Cassie undid the latches and raised the lid. Inside, resting on scraps of faded yellow fabric was a leather journal.

"Rosa used a code for the people she helped," Tessa continued. "Diamonds for the soldiers. Silver for resistance fighters. Pearls for the wealthy, displaced persons—what they paid for their escapes funded so many more, the ones Rosa called her special parcels."

Cassie lifted the journal out and handed it to Drake. It was old, but the leather had been well-oiled, was still soft to touch. Then she saw what the faded yellow fabric scraps were.

Stars. Six-pointed Jewish stars. Yellow and gold, some faded, some with Hebrew letters in the center, others with the word: *Jude.*

Tears fracturing her vision, she carefully took each star, cradling them in her palm one at a time, and laid them out on the coffee table. Forty-nine total.

"Those are Rosa's real treasures," Tessa said. "She and Padraic risked their lives, sneaking into occupied Paris, living like rats in the catacombs beneath the city, came close to being caught by the Gestapo until Rosa led them on a wild goose chase while Padraic spirited their treasure away."

And Rosa ended up killing the man who had betrayed her: Bernard Lavelle, Kasanov's father. That's what started all this, Cassie realized. That and the fact that Bernard never knew what Rosa's gold really was.

Adeena drew close to the coffee table, kneeling beside Cassie to examine the stars. "This is what Kasanov wanted?"

"Fool didn't realize there's things more precious than gold," Tessa scoffed. "This is the treasure Rosa and Paddy smuggled out of Paris on that last trip. Forty-nine children, their parents sent east to the death camps, none older than ten. They were only meant to bring eleven, ones with families here in the States who'd paid for them to be transported."

"But they couldn't leave the others behind," Drake said, leafing through the leather journal.

"No. So they risked everything to bring them all here."

"Why the secrecy?" Cassie asked.

Adeena answered, "In 1940, the States had a lot of anti-Semitism. If they were brought here as orphans, adopted by gentiles, their heritage could have serious repercussions, war or no war."

"Funny to think, but back then, that kind of thing could wreck families, destroy a person's standing in society," Tessa said. "Rosa had Paddy record everything the children could remember about their real families. She kept it safe for them in case they or their children or grandchildren ever wanted the truth."

"Rosa and Paddy never took credit? Never told anyone?" Cassie asked.

"Wasn't their secret to tell," Drake said. He laid a hand on Cassie's shoulder, stroking her hair as he read the journal entries.

"What should we do?" Cassie asked him.

Tessa shifted in her seat. "Rosa said to give it to you and your intended on the day of your wedding. Said between the two of you, you'd know what to do."

"I think the time for secrets is past," Cassie said. "These children deserve to be remembered for who they really are. We should donate these to the Holocaust museum. They can reach out to the children, see what they want."

Drake smiled down at her and nodded his approval.

"As usual, Rosa was right," Tessa said. She flounced back, folding her arms across her chest, giving them a haughty look. "And the wedding isn't cancelled. Why should it be? You're both here, whole and healthy, and so's your mom, Drake." She tsked. "Cancel the wedding? Nonsense."

DRAKE STOOD AT the end of the aisle, waiting for Hart. He'd been right about the weather; a clear night sky with a half moon and a million stars graced them with their light. The roses and other flowers perfumed the gathering inside the canopy as the children, Antwan, Bridget, and Colton, raced up and down the aisle, showering rose petals on anyone who smiled at them.

And there were a lot of smiling people in the crowd. Laughter, too. Which was exactly why he'd done this. Hart could care less about an official ceremony; she believed in action more than words. But he'd wanted—he'd needed—this public affirmation. Not to prove to Hart how much he loved her, rather to proclaim it to the world at large.

Adeena appeared, gave him a smile and nod, and the string quartet began to play music Drake stopped hearing as soon as Hart stepped into view. With a dry cleaner's help, Denise and Adeena had worked magic and Muriel's dress looked almost as good as new. Where they hadn't been able to get the stains out or had to hide their mending, they'd added sprays of freshwater pearls that were a close match to the original ones that trimmed the hem and bodice.

The shoes had become a last-minute panic. The white pumps that matched the dress had been forgotten at Tessa's house. It was doubtful Hart could have worn them anyway with the cuts on her feet, so she'd opted to walk down the aisle barefoot, had even tried to persuade the others it was an old Roma custom.

Then Drake had remembered the Christmas present he'd found while strolling the Strip District. He'd stumbled upon a booth that had lovely silk dancing slippers with hand-sewn beading. He knew they were something Hart would never buy for herself, too impractical. He'd bought a pair in an exquisite shade of mauve that reminded him of the light at sunrise when he'd watched her sleep after their first night together. Turned out, his woefully impractical gift worked beautifully as bridal shoes.

Her former boss, Ed Castro, at her side, more of an escort than a father figure giving her away, Hart strode down the aisle. She wasn't the graceful, gliding bride of movies. Rather, she was certain and confident as she moved toward Drake, her gaze fixed on his.

And then she was there. In front of him. Adeena had pinned a spray of the tiny pearls onto a barrette and fastened it to hide the surgical staples holding Hart's scalp together. Bruises that couldn't be hidden by makeup blossomed over her cheek and chin and one eye was swollen. But she was there. For Drake no bride—no woman—had ever looked as beautiful.

Somehow, he managed to make it through the ceremony without blubbering, although by the end, even Hart's eyes were misted by tears and most people, Jimmy included, were audibly sobbing. These were good tears, though. Tears of joy.

Then it was over. They kissed, the crowd cheered, rose petals floated all around them, and they were bound forever as one.

Hours later, after everyone had eaten and toasted and danced the night away and then gone home again, after the musicians played one more waltz for him and Hart alone as they danced beneath the starlight, he sat with Hart on the roof's parapet, legs dangling over the edge, arms entwined, her head on his shoulder as they looked out at the city's lights.

"Happy?" he asked.

She made the sound a cat does when it's too content to bother purring and nuzzled her face against the crook of his neck. "Ecstatic." She kicked her feet gleefully. "These are the most comfortable shoes I've ever worn. I'm never taking them off."

He turned his face to hers and stole a kiss. "We'll see about that."

"I wish it could always be this way. I want to take this one perfect night and put it in a snow globe, keep it forever."

"We'll have it forever. And we can make as many nights like this one as we want."

"That's right. We can." She turned her face up, the light and her grin giving her a childlike innocence. Except for her eyes. She had her grandmother's eyes, ancient beyond her years.

Drake was pleased to see that tonight, in this moment, even those solemn, serious eyes gleamed with a smile.
"We can do anything. As long as we have each other."

NOTE TO READERS

Thanks for reading EYE OF THE STORM! I hope you enjoyed Hart & Drake's wedding story and Rosa and Padraic's adventures in France.

A quick note on the historical facts. Varian Fry, mentioned briefly in EYE OF THE STORM, is a true hero who was responsible for rescuing thousands from Marseilles. He worked with an eclectic team including Albert Hirschman, who infamously said, "I always make it a practice to clear out when the head of a fascist state comes to town."

Varian and his team were imprisoned on the *Senaia,* as were six hundred other potential "troublemakers" when Marshal Petain visited Marseilles on an inspection tour. Unlike the fictional version of the *Senaia* presented here, the real ship remained docked until Petain departed the city three days later.

There were several rescue routes run by the French and Belgium Resistance, including one run by a girl almost as young as Rosa. Andrée Eugénie Adrienne De Jongh was in her early twenties when she established the Comet line that saved over four hundred people. She was eventually imprisoned in Villa Chagrin, Fresnes, and Ravensbruck.

Also, a group of daring, young Americans did use a purloined ambulance to whisk captured British soldiers and French Resistance fighters from Gestapo- and Vichy-run prison hospitals—not once, but several times. They also worked with Varian Fry for a time.

To learn more about Varian Fry and his adventures, read *A Hero of Our Own* by Sheila Isenberg. More information about the Roma's entanglements with the Nazis can be found in *The Nazi Persecution of the Gypsies* by Guenter Lewy.

For the purposes of fiction, I have changed many of the situations and none of the characters are based on any real-life person other than historical figures who are mentioned briefly.

Want advance notice of my next Thriller with Heart? Sign up for my newsletter at CJLyons.net

As always, thanks for reading!

CJ

ABOUT CJ

New York Times and *USA Today* bestselling author of twenty-nine novels, former pediatric ER doctor CJ Lyons has lived the life she writes about in her cutting edge Thrillers with Heart.

CJ has been called a "master within the genre" (Pittsburgh Magazine) and her work has been praised as "breathtakingly fast-paced" and "riveting" (Publishers Weekly) with "characters with beating hearts and three dimensions" (Newsday).

Her novels have won the International Thriller Writers' prestigious Thriller Award, the RT Reviewers' Choice Award, the Readers' Choice Award, the RT Seal of Excellence, and the Daphne du Maurier Award for Excellence in Mystery and Suspense.

Learn more about CJ's Thrillers with Heart at www.CJLyons.net